S0-AFN-692

Sanctuary

Molly Brown

For Steve
Live the dream
of the earth!

Molly Brown

Copyright ©2016 Molly Brown

Sanctuary
Sanctuaryearth.wordpress.com
Mollybee1173@gmail.com

Available from Amazon.com and other book stores

All Rights Reserved.

Printed in the USA

This book is a work of fiction.

Cover art and interior art ©2016 Molly Brown

The earth will solve its problems, and possibly
our own . . .

Thomas Berry
The Dream of the Earth

1

Flying low over the peninsula, the Cessna Skyhawk shuddered in the wind and banked to the right. The pilot guided the plane in a wide, bumpy circle as Marvin Younger took pictures from the window.

Jim Oakley leaned across the seat to look out the window and shouted over the churning engine and buffeting wind. "How's it look?"

"It's coming along," Younger shouted back. "Looks like we're more or less on schedule."

The sandy peninsula stretched out below them, twelve miles of forested dunes ending at its northern tip in a big sand bar hooking back into the bay. To the west, Pacific Ocean breakers washed the long, sandy beach. To the east, low tide exposed river-like channels curving through the mud of the bay where wind ruffled the shallow water into whitecaps.

The main road ran south to north for the length of the narrow peninsula, passing through a little town at its midpoint. A mile north of the town a side road branched west toward the ocean beach, ending at a cluster of houses below the center of the Skyhawk's circle. A bulldozer pushed sand from the beach below, working it into a berm between the houses and a little creek that drained a nearby marsh.

The plane skidded sideways in the wind, making Younger curse as he tried to hold the camera steady, pointing it at the bulldozer.

"Is he doing what he's supposed to be doing?"

Oakley shrugged. "As far as I know he is." A sudden gust shook the plane, making Younger's camera bang against the window.

"Where did they find him anyway? Is he an actual employee of SeaMist?" Oakley asked.

Younger glanced at Oakley and raised a warning eyebrow. "He's worked for SeaMist on a few projects. Sort of a handyman. Valuable skill set . . ."

The plane dropped like an elevator a couple hundred feet. The pilot fought the wind to bring it back up.

". . . but he's not the kind of employee you want to have on the books."

Oakley nodded and gripped the back of the seat as the plane slid sideways again. Younger cursed.

"He has a reputation for being impatient," Oakley said.

"And a reputation for being a genius. At certain things."

The plane dipped again and leaped up, jerking like a kite. The pilot glanced over his shoulder at the passengers as he worked to keep it on course. "There's a big storm coming in," he shouted. "Getting way too windy up here. Got to set it down."

"We're done." Younger gave a thumbs up and pointed in the direction of the airport.

The Skyhawk banked and headed south. Below them, between the main road and the beach, a grass fire burned in the dunes.

2

"Hey Oakley," Younger shouted, "Shouldn't you be down there?"

Oakley laughed and winked. "Mahoney can take care of it."

* * *

Assistant Fire Chief Mick Mahoney turned down the volume on his fire band scanner as he slid into a booth at the Crow's Nest. He ordered coffee and rhubarb pie, then flipped his checkbook onto the table. Shaking his head in self-reproach, he wrote out a check to Puget Sound Fidelity. Until several months ago the family land had never borne any kind of lien. And now Mick had borrowed money on it. Hearing what Mick had done, the Cranberry Beach librarian had informed him that the word mortgage had the literal meaning of "death pledge."

It must have been nothing but her bookish appreciation of words that prompted this observation but it stuck in Mick's chest like heartburn. The land, sixty-eight acres of ocean beach, pasture, cranberry bogs, tidelands and woods, had been homesteaded more than a hundred years before by Mick's great-grandfather and worked by his grandfather and father before Mick inherited it. They had all weathered their own hard times without selling any of the land.

The mortgage was a gamble but it had been the only solution he could come up with. Julie wanted her half of the community property settlement immediately, back taxes had to be paid, and Sean needed help getting back on the right track. The mortgage gave him the money he needed right away. All he had to do was wait until the real estate market improved, then sell fifteen or twenty acres of prime beachfront to pay off the loan. Which would likely be soon. He hoped. Rumor floated around that a real estate development company had been eyeing the peninsula lately.

But no one on the peninsula had gotten an offer yet. And he had only enough money in the bank to pay the mortgage for two more months.

The scanner squawked on his belt. It was only law enforcement chatter but he turned up the volume to listen as he licked the envelope and stuck on a stamp.

Sherry put down his coffee and pie and wiped her fingers on her apron.

"That about the storm?" she asked, nodding her head toward the scanner. She picked up the cash he had put on the table.

"Yeah," he said. "Might be another big one, but then again might fizzle out like the last one. Weather service isn't calling it yet."

Wind banged the screen door against the jamb, tossing in a gritty handful of beach sand.

"It's weird to have a storm when it's so hot," Sherry said, her round face flushed and beaded with sweat. She leaned out the door to look up at the hazy sky and frowned as a small plane buzzed low overhead.

"Now who the hell is that?" she said.

Mick glanced out the window but couldn't see the plane. He stirred two packets of sugar and two creams into his coffee.

"How can you drink that hot coffee today?" Sherry slid into the seat across from him. It was three o'clock, almost the end of her shift.

"Habit," Mick answered, uneasily aware of his recently divorced status.

Sherry sat with her elbows on the table, chin propped on the heels of her hands, looking at him expectantly. She probably wanted conversation. A little rivulet of sweat ran down her neck and disappeared in the plump line of her cleavage. She was a widow. Her husband had been killed a few years ago in one of the endless Middle East wars. Everybody knew she was looking for someone. For Mick the idea of dating again was disconcerting.

He dug into the tart, sweet pie which she had warmed in the microwave.

"Do you like that pie?"

"Yeah. It's good."

Julie had wanted conversation too. But her emotions always got in the way. Whenever they talked she ended up sad or angry.

4

His suggestions that she get medical care for her depression insulted her. In time he fell into the habit of mentally turning her off. So it was a stinging surprise when, after more than forty years of marriage, a process server handed him divorce papers across the counter at the Mercantile.

The scanner emitted a pattern of tones as the dispatcher's voice dispassionately gave details of a fire call. Mick finished the pie in three big bites and gulped half his coffee while scooting out of the booth.

"Whatcha got?" Sherry called after him as he bounded out the door.

"Dune grass fire," he shouted back to her.

Mick tossed the mortgage payment into a mail collection box at the front door of the Crow's Nest. He loped the three blocks to the fire station, went in the side door and slapped the switch that opened the engine bay doors. Prying off his shoes, he stepped through his neatly pre-positioned bunker pants into his boots, pulled the pants up and slipped the wide red suspenders over his shoulders.

Volunteer firefighters Joe DeLorme and Jimmy Whittaker charged through the side door together, Don Tenney three seconds behind.

Mick shrugged into his turnout coat and grabbed his helmet from the shelf.

Whittaker, younger than Mick by three decades and way more agile, had already gotten into his gear, taken the driver position in the pumper truck and kicked the engine into a gratifying racket by the time Mick climbed into the cab and picked up the radio to report to dispatch they were on the way. Two seconds later he heard DeLorme's voice on the radio reporting the tanker truck was also underway. Sirens wailing and lights flashing, the two orange firetrucks turned left onto the main highway and roared south.

A mile and a half south of town they turned onto a sandy beach access road. A small fire blew through the dune grass on twenty-mile-per-hour south winds. They were lucky. The access road would be an effective fire break, though they would need to get water on the fire quickly.

5

Mick looked around for the fire chief's car among the dozen or so private vehicles driven to the scene by volunteer firefighters.

"Anybody heard from Oakley?"

Nobody had. Mick, as he did more often than not these days, took charge.

*　*　*

Playing in the sand, nine-year-old Amanda noticed neither the smoke from the fire three miles down the beach nor the bulldozer working near the cottages. Her attention was wholly involved in the examination of a tiny, wrecked body that lay nearly buried in the sand, tangled in the high tide line of seaweed and plastic debris. With a stick she propped the creature up and gazed into the sand-encrusted hole where the dangling head had formerly joined the body.

Bending close enough to smell its rotting garbage odor, she poked the stick a half inch into the neck hole. Withdrawing it, she studied the greenish black gore, wiped it off in the sand, and inserted the stick in the hole again. This time she pressed harder, forcing the stick in as far as it would go.

With both hands holding the stick she picked up the impaled leathery creature and examined the four flippers, stiff as jerky, the plated, shoe leather back, the nearly decapitated head with its pinhole nostrils and desiccated eyes, and the mouth with its cute overbite.

"Amanda—I can't *see* you."

The girl set the creature down, moved around a driftwood log, stepped into her mother's line of sight and waved. "I'm over here Mom."

Her mother waved back from a lounge chair where she sat reading, sheltered by low dunes from the wind and the noise of the bulldozer. The big black dog at her side stopped scratching his armpits at the sound of the child's voice and galloped toward Amanda, long fur bouncing like a dust mop.

Amanda used the stick to lift the creature onto a driftwood log. She found a fist-sized rock and tapped it once on the hard, rounded back. Swinging the stone again with force, she broke the shell. Stinky fluid spattered on her hand. She wiped it on her shorts.

The dog arrived, sportive and curious. Amanda pushed him away with her hip.

"Go away, Joey." The dog lay down and rolled onto his back, begging a tummy rub, but she ignored him.

With a seagull feather she probed the shell fragments, moving them aside to reveal the internal organs. Flies buzzed around the cadaver. She slid the feather in, drew out glistening bits of viscera and laid them out on the driftwood.

Joey thrust his nose into the operating field and sniffed. Amanda slapped him and pushed him away with her elbow. He backed off, circled around, and edged in again. Amanda used both hands to push him away, causing the creature to slide off the log.

The dog dove for it, snatched it up in his mouth, and romped away, eluding Amanda's grasp. He pranced ahead of her, tossing his head to send the creature tumbling in the air. He scooped it up again just as Amanda grabbed a handful of hair on the back of his neck.

"Drop that, you sonofabitch."

"AMANDA!" Her mother got out of the lounge chair and looked for her shoes.

A tiny black flipper protruded from under the dog's lip. Amanda tried to force his mouth open but Joey kept it clamped shut even though she slapped his nose.

She whispered into the dog's ear, "Shit on a shingle, you poop head. Let go of it."

Joey held tight, drooling. A growl gargled in the back of his throat.

"Mom. MOM. Make him let go!"

Amanda kept a strangle hold on Joey's collar until her mother got there.

"He's eating it," Amanda said. "Make him spit it out."

The woman lifted the dog's lips, exposing a portion of shell and a flipper between the clenched teeth. She tried to pry his jaws open but his snarl deterred her.

"Oh, for Pete's sake, Joey. Don't eat that. It's decomposed." Under her breath she muttered, "I hate dogs."

Amanda kicked him in the ribs.

"No, Amanda. Don't hurt him."

Joey dropped the creature and both he and Amanda dove for it. There was a crunching sound, the dog choked and hacked, gulped and swallowed.

Amanda sat hunched on the sand wailing. "It was a sea turtle, Mom!"

"It couldn't have been, 'Manda Bear, not here on the Washington coast. The water's too cold. They live in warm places, like Hawaii. It was probably only a crab."

"But it had flippers. It was a swimming turtle."

"And anyway, it was much too small to be a sea turtle."

"It was a baby one."

Glaring at the dog, the woman said, "I hope he doesn't throw up on the carpet again. Stupid thing."

Joey smiled up at her and wagged his tail, pleased to be the center of attention.

Amanda's mom squinted against the wind driven sand to watch the bulldozer. "When is he going to be done with that?"

To Amanda she said, "Don't play with dead things on the beach. How many times do I have to tell you that? Come on, I've got some antibacterial hand cleanser in my bag."

* * *

By five o'clock that afternoon the atmospheric haze had thickened to an iron gray murk. The last wind speed update reported on the scanner was thirty-five miles per hour. Gale force. Not uncommon on the peninsula, but the main part of the storm wasn't supposed to hit land for several more hours.

In the back room of the Cranberry Beach Mercantile, Mick tightened down the last screws on the sheriff's chainsaw. He wiped it clean and took it to the counter where the sheriff was shooting the breeze with Don Tenney and Jimmy Whittaker while he waited for the repair.

"I put a new gasket on that carburetor but I don't know how long it's going to work," Mick said. "Let's hope you don't have to use it tonight. It needs a complete overhaul, more than I can do here." He opened a tattered spiral notebook marked "Sheriff Dept. Account" and recorded the cost.

Sheriff Grayson gave a short bark of laughter. "What it really needs is to be new. But hell, the county can't afford to replace anything, not even me, and I'm a helluva lot older than this chainsaw."

Grayson's belly strained at his shirt buttons as he laughed at his own joke. The others laughed with him.

"By the way, good work—all of you—on that dune fire this afternoon," he said.

Jimmy grinned. "Good *luck* was all it was. If the wind had been coming off the west like usual that fire could have been into the pines and burned all the way over to the bay by now."

"Those tourists were awful sorry their beach fire got away from them," the sheriff said, laughing. "The lady was crying and the man was running around waving his credit card yelling 'I'll take care of any damages!'"

The men guffawed and slapped the counter.

"Did you write them a citation?" Don asked.

"Hell yes. But I should have arrested them for ignoring all those signs about no burning of any kind anywhere on this peninsula."

Mick looked out the window at the pasty, glowering sky. "Maybe this storm will give us a good rain." He reached up to turn on the TV for the latest weather report.

A young woman and little girl wearing summer dresses and flip flops came into the Mercantile and went to the ice cream freezer. Their big black dog stood panting in the doorway with his front toes

9

on the threshold, technically not in the store. His lolling tongue dripped a puddle on the wood plank floor.

The woman brought two ice cream bars to the counter and dug money out of her purse. "So what do you think about the storm?" she asked Mick as he rang up her purchase.

She handed one ice cream to her daughter, peeled the paper off the other one and nibbled on the chocolate coating.

Mick indicated the TV with a nod as he counted out her change. "The weather reports aren't saying much. But just going by how strong the wind is already, I wouldn't be surprised if we had a pretty good blow tonight."

The sheriff's radio burped out an undecipherable message. Grayson thumbed the volume down. "Surf might come up higher than usual too," he said. "Risky for people on the beach. And the power could go out. Do you have candles?"

"I'll get some," she said. "But we're staying in the cottages on the dunes. Maybe we shouldn't be so close to the surf if it's going to get high."

"Oh, I wouldn't worry about being in the cottages, the surf could never get up that far," Grayson said. "But if it does start to look even a little questionable, one of the deputies or one of these volunteer firemen will come and let you and the other folks out there know. Don't worry, all of us in emergency services are going to be up watching this storm all night."

With a reassuring smile for the young woman, Sheriff Grayson picked up his chainsaw and headed for the door. He paused in front of the dog who was blocking the exit. "Excuse me," he said.

The dog looked up at him, reeled in his tongue, and backed up three steps, making just enough room for the Sheriff to get around him. Then he returned to his place on the threshold and let his dripping tongue out again.

The woman and girl finished their ice cream and tossed the wrappers in the trash. When the mother picked up a shopping basket and moved out of sight in the grocery aisles, the little girl approached the counter and caught Mick's eye. Her dark hair was pulled up off her neck and sloppily fastened with a big, brightly painted clip

10

shaped like a butterfly. She wore a red Hawaiian print shift. Standing on tiptoes she extended her hand for Mick to shake and in a serious and businesslike way said, "Hello, I'm Amanda."

Mick leaned over the counter to take the small, sticky hand and gave it a gentle shake. "I'm Mick. How can I help you?"

"Well," Amanda said, "I have a question for you."

"Shoot," Mick said, grinning. Don and Jimmy smiled.

"Sea turtles," Amanda said, "Are they found on this beach?"

"No, they can't live this far north. It's too cold."

"Ever?"

"Oh, every now and then one washes up on the beach. Sometimes a storm will blow one off course and it gets stranded. But they're usually pretty close to dead by the time they get here. They live in the ocean in southern latitudes where it's very warm."

"It's warm here now," Amanda said.

"This isn't how it usually is."

"I found one on the beach today," Amanda said. "Mom said it was a crab." She turned to point accusingly at the dog. "Joey ate it."

Mick smiled and tried not to laugh. "It must have been pretty small."

"This big." Amanda took a folded piece of paper from her dress pocket and smoothed it open on the counter. "I drew it exactly."

Mick examined the amazingly detailed drawing which clearly showed flippers and not the toed feet of a common land turtle. Don and Jimmy leaned over to get a look too.

"It was a baby one," Amanda said.

"This is a very good drawing," Mick said, "but I don't know how such a small sea turtle could be on our beach. As far as I know they nest very far away in Central America." Except for the detail of the severed neck, Mick thought she might have copied the drawing from an encyclopedia.

He scratched his chin, enduring Amanda's gaze.

"Tell you what," he said. "I know someone around here who is interested in turtles. When I see her again, I'll tell her what you saw."

"Amanda, don't bother the man," her mother said, hefting her basket onto the counter. She smiled at Mick. "It was a crab."

Amanda frowned at her mother, folded the drawing and put it back in the pocket of her dress.

When they had gone Jimmy shook his head and laughed. "How the hell hot does it have to be to hatch sea turtles?"

"It's a freaking strange summer, you can't dispute that," Don said. He went out on the porch and checked the thermometer. "Ninety-one. And it's cloudy. How do you explain that?"

"The wind's blowing sand across the dunes like buckshot," Jimmy said. "That's why we had to quit early today."

"Oakley send you home?" Mick asked.

"Nah, we haven't seen the boss yet today," Jimmy said. He held his vintage Van Halen T-shirt out to catch cool air from the fan, showing the flat, muscled abdomen naturally acquired by young men who work at physical labor. Both Jimmy and Don wore khaki shorts and scuffed workboots, their skin was deeply tanned, their hair sun-bleached, the tops of their noses sunburned and peeling.

"He's probably playing golf someplace nice," Don snickered.

"How's the surf look?"

"Big," Jimmy said. "I'm surprised we haven't gotten a surf rescue call today."

Don laughed. "Maybe our signs are working. Scary enough to keep the ones that can't swim out of the water anyway."

Jimmy grinned. "You mean that sign that says 'Great White Sharks Have Been Spotted Here Recently'?"

"Very effective, don't you think?"

Jimmy went to rummage in the beer cooler.

"Does Oakley still have Boris running the bulldozer on the beach?" Mick asked Don.

"Yeah, though what the hell he's doing is beyond me. He's pushing sand out of the little cove where Decker Creek empties onto the beach and shoving it up around the cottages."

12

"Some kind of erosion control, I would guess," Mick said.

"The way these storms have been cutting into the beach, all that sand will probably be gone by this time tomorrow," Don said.

Jimmy slid a dewy six-pack of cold beer onto the counter and laid down a twenty-dollar bill.

"What the hell is Boris's real name anyway?" he asked.

They had tagged him with the name of the short, surly Russian no-goodnik from the '70s Rocky and Bullwinkle cartoon.

"You mean Boris Badenov?" Don tipped his head toward the door. "Why don't you ask him?"

A short, lean, balding man strode into the Mercantile more vigorously than the hot weather would warrant and went straight back to the electrical supply section. The three men standing around the counter exchanged glances with each other.

A few minutes later the man they called Boris dumped several packages of electrical connectors, a roll of copper wire, a roll of black electrical tape, and three thick, long-shafted drill bits onto the counter. Mick bagged the items as he keyed them into the cash register.

"That'll be $74.24."

Boris pulled cash from his wallet, keeping an eye on the TV weather report.

Digging an elbow into Jimmy's ribs, Don gave him an encouraging nod.

"Uh, hello there," Jimmy said, waving to catch Boris's attention.

Boris looked at Jimmy and shrugged.

Jimmy held out his hand to shake and said, "Hi, I'm Jimmy Whittaker and this is my friend Don Tenney."

Bowing slightly and looking irritated, Boris briefly shook hands with each of them.

"And this is Mick Mahoney," Jimmy said, gesturing toward Mick.

With an expression more grimace than smile, Boris shook Mick's hand.

"What's your name?" Jimmy asked. He pointed to himself and said, "Jimmy," then at the other two men saying, "Don, Mick." Then he pointed at Boris and said, "What's *your* name?"

Boris shrugged and shook his head.

Jimmy started the pointing again but Boris interrupted in a guttural foreign language with a fluent statement that sounded like it might have some profanity in it.

Jimmy shrugged this time. "Sorry, I don't understand."

Boris took a card out of his wallet and waved it at them. Saying something that sounded like 'Green card, legal' in thickly accented English, he scowled and pointed to himself then picked up his bag and stalked out the door.

The three men watched as he climbed into a tan SUV and slammed it into gear. His tires threw up gravel as he swung out of the parking lot.

"What the hell was that? Russian?" Don asked, grinning.

Jimmy laughed. "Hell, everybody knows he's Russian, probably ex-KGB."

"Doesn't he live up at Oakley's house?" Mick asked.

"Yeah, in an apartment in the garage." Jimmy said.

"Well, did you ever ask Oakley what Boris's name is?"

"Nah."

* * *

The overhead lights in the Mercantile flickered about seven o'clock. Bev, back from her dinner break, looked at Mick over the tops of her glasses and raised her eyebrows. He turned the volume up on the TV so they could hear the latest from the Weather Channel.

The satellite image showed what looked like a giant cotton ball nudging the Northwest coast. A meteorologist drew glowing arrows over the map and gabbed about pressure gradients. An intense extra-tropical cyclone, he called it. When asked how serious and damaging the storm would be, he avoided saying anything definite. There had been too many missed predictions lately, a consequence of lapsed government funding of weather data systems and a broken coastal radar. And recently a few satellites had been knocked off line by sunspot activity. The big media companies behind TV forecasting no longer wanted to stick their necks out and risk losing viewers. So the meteorologist would only say that the weather service was waiting for more data before issuing severe storm warnings. At this point they were forecasting strong winds and high surf on the coast and would update hourly.

"I talked with Reenie this afternoon," Bev said. "Her cousin called. The one who works in the Weather Service office in Portland. He says this storm is looking like trouble but they can't see how much rain is in it because the coastal radar is down again. And the weather buoys aren't all reporting either. But they're thinking it might be strong enough to bring on a storm surge and flooding in low-lying areas. Some even want to call an evacuation along the coast, though they can't tell where or when the storm's going to come ashore. But at the same time they're afraid it might not amount to anything and calling an evacuation would get everyone mad at them. So they're not doing anything yet. Anyway, he told Reenie she should take the kids and visit her relatives in Chehalis for a couple days."

"Evacuate—like they do in Florida when a hurricane's coming?"

"Yeah. How many folks do you think are on the peninsula this week?"

"Too many to evacuate unless they started yesterday."

Bev limped over to the door. "It's sure as hell making my arthritis ache. And would you look at that sky. Weird."

Mick went out on the porch and looked up at a strangely pink and shimmering atmosphere. Something to do with the angle of the setting sun, he guessed.

"He mentioned a storm surge?" Flooding had been a growing problem on the peninsula lately.

"Yep." Bev picked up one of the folding chairs and leaned it against the wall inside the Mercantile. Mick gathered up the rest and brought them in.

"I think we better take everything inside tonight," Bev said.

The wind tinkered with all the moving parts of the Mercantile as Mick went around closing shutters and stowing loose things, making the two-story clapboard building as weather tight as if it were November.

The sturdy post and beam structure had served as the center of commerce in Cranberry Beach since the 1920s, in its early days a cranberry packing plant. Later it expanded into groceries and hardware as the little town grew. Bev and Merle had run the business since the sixties, earning a comfortable living for most of those years. But by the time Merle died, government rules and corporate expediencies had deflated the cranberry market. Prosperity declined on the peninsula and now business at the Mercantile was slow.

Once in a while Mick had to wait an extra week or two for his paycheck. Years ago he had gone into one of the big home improvement stores in Astoria, looking for a better job. But the application form had stopped him short. A certain box to check and a line that asked for details. He had wadded the paper and tossed it into the trash on his way out.

After that he never thought much about leaving the Mercantile for a better job. He had done this one too long, was used to it, liked it. And Bev needed him, not only to wait on customers and stock shelves, but for all the little maintenance things and repairs Merle used to do. He liked the fire department too, though there was no paycheck for the assistant chief position.

But the mortgage company had approved his loan anyway and hadn't expressed much concern that he could pay it back with his meager and inconsistent salary. It was all in the collateral, they had said.

He kicked a rock under one of the feet of the extension ladder to level it, then climbed to a set of second story windows to close and fasten the storm shutters. A warm, driving wind flapped at his shirt, making the ladder lurch and inch sideways against the siding.

Winter was when the big storms usually blew off the Pacific, but this summer and the two before, several warm, windy and wet systems had lashed the coast in August and September. People on the peninsula had resisted the idea of global warming for years. In the beginning the science had been confusing and the politics contentious, but now evidence that ordinary people could believe was turning up all the time. The Pacific Ocean, usually bone chilling, had gotten remarkably warm. The weather was undeniably different. And some strange things had been washing up on the beach. Coconuts from Hawaii. A dead sailfish.

He went inside and gathered a few groceries, things that wouldn't need refrigeration in case the power went out. Bev rang them up.

"I'll do the rest of the closing," she said. "Go now so you can get some supper before they start calling you out to deal with storm damage."

"I'm going to see if I can find the Turtle Lady before it gets dark," he said. "I saw her out at the point a day ago."

"That crazy woman who lives on the beach?"

"I don't think she's crazy, she just does what she wants," Mick said.

"You're a kind person." Bev regarded him with a warm smile.

"Not really," Mick said lightly, dodging the praise. "It's just that I sure wouldn't want to be out on the beach in a storm like this."

"No," Bev said, planting her age-spotted, gnarled hand on Mick's forearm for emphasis. "You really are kind. I've been meaning to tell you how much I admire you. And Merle thought the world of you. Everybody in Cranberry Beach does. You've done so much for this community in your own way. Fixing somebody's washing machine or chopping fire wood for an old lady. All those things you do without thinking about it. And with everything that's happened to you lately, the divorce and Sean's troubles, well, I just want to say there's no way you've deserved it . . ." She sputtered to a stop, her wrinkled cheeks flushed and eyes teary.

Mick felt a familiar queasy wave of guilt as he gathered up his groceries. If she knew the truth about him she probably wouldn't feel that way. None of them would.

"Thanks for your support, Bev," he said, and turned away, ashamed.

2

Wind rattled the windows of the rented beach cottage as Amanda watched her mother take two entrees out of the microwave and peel the cellophane off the tops.

"Oh yuck. What the *hell* is that?" Amanda sniffed suspiciously at the steaming food.

"Amanda." Her mother frowned. "That is not acceptable language and you know it."

Amanda stabbed a gravy covered slab of chicken and lifted it to her nose. "Dad talks that way," she said.

"Dad is not the best of role models."

"Where is Dad anyway? I thought he was supposed to be here by now."

"Oh . . . he couldn't get off work. But I just had to . . . I mean, we needed to get away and have a little vacation even if he couldn't come."

Amanda was quiet for a minute, digging a hole in her mashed potatoes. "Did he go over to Dee Dee's house again?"

Her mother's face turned pale. "What are you talking about?"

"You argue very *loudly*. I can hear even when I'm asleep, you know."

"Never mind about that. It's nothing you should be concerned with." She poured another glass of wine, slopping some onto the table. "Let's get off this subject."

"Okay," Amanda shrugged and went back to sculpting her potatoes. "Here's a good question. Intestines." She glanced at her mother.

"What about them?"

"What are they?"

Her mother laughed in a relieved way. "They're inside your tummy. They're internal organs."

"Does everything have them?"

"I think most things do."

"Does Joey have them?"

"Yes."

"Do bugs have them?"

"I think so."

Thoughtful silence. "Do sea turtles have them?"

"Yes, I think all animals have them."

"What do they look like?"

"Long, ropey things all coiled up inside the tummy."

"Hmmm."

"Eat your dinner please."

"Okay." Amanda gnawed a big bite off the piece of chicken and talked with her mouth full. "Here's another question."

Amanda's mother tipped her glass up to drain it, an extra-large mouthful.

"Divorce . . ."

She choked on the wine.

" . . . what is it?" Amanda asked.

* * *

Mick went out to the parking lot, fumbling with the unfamiliar key fob for his new red Suburban. He had gotten into the habit of locking it to protect the fancy emergency gear he had installed to make it a somewhat official fire department vehicle. It was useful to have the red lights under the front grille and the siren and communication gear, but actually he traveled to most of the fire calls in one of the fire trucks.

He glanced at the aged but reliable Chevy pickup he had driven for years—and never had to lock—parked now in the back of the Mercantile. It had been a good truck and served him well. Nothing was seriously wrong with it.

But when he had taken out the loan and written out checks for Julie and Sean, he had gone and put a down payment on this expensive new vehicle as a present for himself. He didn't really understand why he had bought it, but owning this fancy thing had turned out to be more worry than pleasure for him. He ought to sell it back to the dealer before he ran out of money to pay for it.

Mick pulled onto the highway under a sky blackening with the approaching storm. A handful of raindrops burst like water balloons on the windshield, making a concrete slurry of the fine sand the ocean wind had deposited there. He cycled the windshield washers, leaning forward to peer through the mud as he drove, thinking about how to find Anna Davis, the Turtle Lady.

He had seen her yesterday when he had been on beach safety patrol just south of the point. She had roamed the beaches of this peninsula for the past three summers, camping and beachcombing with her little black and white dog. Mick had talked with her a few times and didn't think, as most of the other locals did, that she was crazy. It was just that the wind tangled her thick white hair and her blue eyes were a little startling in the lined, tan skin of her face and she was over seventy and not afraid to be alone and out of doors. She was a biologist looking for sea turtles along the peninsula, though it was impossibly far north of their normal range. Perhaps it was an unrealistic quest but Mick knew plenty of "normal" people who did equally pointless things.

No doubt she could take care of herself in most situations, but the weather forecast was bad and getting worse every hour. Though August was usually a time of gentle weather, the storm sweeping off the Pacific was shaping up to be as violent as anything that had ever smashed into the coast in November. Most of the tourists and campers had moved off the beach, away from the worst of the wind. Some huddled in motorhomes or cabins, avoiding the long crawling queue of vehicles heading off the peninsula. But Mick was afraid

Anna might try to ride it out in some kind of homemade shelter in the dunes.

Driving past the Golden Sands RV Park, just north of Cranberry Beach, Mick saw that it was packed, which worried him. The flooding and erosion of the storm surge, if there was one, would be a problem because most of the peninsula was only a few feet above sea level. Some of the most popular areas for tourists, including the Golden Sands, lay in the lowest elevations.

He passed one of the tsunami evacuation route signs that dotted the peninsula, graphically conveying the danger of earthquake-generated tidal waves. They directed people toward the spine of the peninsula where the elevation reached fifteen feet above sea level in a few places, which was probably not high enough to protect them. The memory of TV pictures of Indonesian and Japanese tsunamis made him shudder. Maybe now people would be more likely to head for higher ground off the peninsula after an earthquake, though the traffic jam would be a nightmare. But the kind of flooding Mick anticipated tonight wouldn't be preceded by shaking ground.

No decision had been made yet about an evacuation of the peninsula in spite of the fact that surface wind speed now occasionally spiked to fifty miles per hour. The weather service was still not sure how bad it was going to get. Peninsula merchants protested the idea of an evacuation because they didn't want to lose tourist dollars. And the sheriff's department was concerned about the logistics of moving several thousand vehicles through the bottleneck of the one highway off the peninsula. But even if no evacuation was called and flooding was minimal, the fire department would surely have a lot on their hands tonight. Downed power lines, trees falling on houses, heart attacks, and whatever else. He would be needed. He listened to the squawking radio scanner as he drove and hoped it wouldn't take too much time to find the Turtle Lady.

A mile down the main highway, Rutter Road angled off to the left along Decker Creek to the dunes and the cottages. Mick thought about going out to check on Amanda and her mom but decided to do it on the way back. He caught a glimpse of what looked like Boris's tan SUV partially hidden in the brush beside the road and wondered what he was up to. Probably some task Oakley wanted done before the storm hit. Mick was in too much of a hurry to think about it.

He slowed to turn into his driveway opposite Rutter Road but decided against that too. Later, on the way back from the point, he would first check on the cottages, then swing by his house and fasten the shutters. The sturdy farmhouse his great grandfather had built in the early 1900s had weathered everything the Pacific Ocean had thrown its way in the last century so there was no reason to worry about it. Maybe he would invite the Turtle Lady to make herself comfortable there for the duration of the storm while he was out on emergency calls.

He drove two miles further on blacktop and then turned left onto a beach access road. He guided the four-wheel-drive Suburban to the beach through sand drifted by the wind onto the gravel road. It was four hours before high tide and he could see waves already breaking far up on the beach. He couldn't chance a run in the Suburban along the hard-packed sand of the beach though that would have been the quickest way to the point. With the tide coming up this fast there was no guarantee there would still be drivable beach on the run home. He watched the breakers for a few minutes, judging some of them to be twenty-footers, spindrift flying from their crests like smoke.

Several young people ran shrieking and laughing through a three-foot layer of white, foamy spume the breakers had deposited along the beach. A Labrador retriever dove repeatedly into the foam, completely disappearing in it and leaping out to the delight of his human companions. Mick drove up to them and got their attention with a little whoop of his siren as he rolled down his window.

"You kids have a car?" Mick shouted into the wind.

One of the boys pointed to a minivan parked on the beach about a quarter mile south.

"You may want to move it to the road before long. And watch the surf, you guys. It's really dangerous. When it's like this it can toss logs way up on the beach."

"Logs?" One of the girls looked blank.

Mick pointed to the silvered driftwood logs piled like pick-up-sticks along the upper beach. "How do you think those got there?"

"Oh." Understanding widened her eyes.

"It would be best if you got off the beach," Mick said, though he knew his advice would be ignored.

He turned back onto the peninsula's only highway. The parking lot of the state park lay five miles north of Cranberry Beach and about a mile south of the tip of the peninsula, depending on how big the ever-shifting sand bars were at any particular point in time. It would take a few minutes to drive to the park. He would hike the mile or so out to the beach, then which way to turn? He would think about that when he got there.

Pastures, shabby farmhouses and weathered cabins decorated with beachcombing finds blurred past as Mick hurried north. He smiled and waved as several cars he recognized as belonging to his neighbors passed him heading in the opposite direction, toward Cranberry Beach and most likely off the peninsula. It didn't take an evacuation order to convince the locals this was no ordinary storm.

The scanner, set to pick up law enforcement as well as fire department communications squawked out a steady play-by-play as the sheriff's department and State Patrol dealt with the growing traffic snarl-up on the highway. Mick figured they would be calling him soon to help out with traffic control and any storm-related problems that were sure to come up.

He pushed the Suburban to fifty-five miles per hour on the two-lane road and reached to turn on the red emergency lights. Then reconsidered. It was not really an emergency, he was just in a hurry. He could turn them on if he got behind somebody.

He heard a scraping concussion as the wind tumbled a fir branch as thick as a baseball bat across the hood. He slowed to turn onto Mendenhall Road and accelerated again. Firs and alders on either side of the road bowed in the wind, flinging showers of twigs and seed cones onto the roof. Though a heavy vehicle, the Suburban veered and swayed in the wind. Working to keep it on the road, he leaned forward to try to see what damage the branch had caused. A dent dimpled the middle of the hood and he could see a divot in the red paint. Maybe I can fix it myself, he thought. Tap the dent out from the inside, spread on a little putty, sand out the scratch. Maybe I can use the paint booth at the body shop . . .

"Jesus!" Mick ducked as a branch whirled toward his face and stabbed the windshield. A star-shaped chip and a long crack appeared in the glass.

A thin fir tree sprawled across the road at the entrance to the park. Mick slowed and walked the Suburban over it, steering gingerly as the branches brushed along the undercarriage. It was a damned lot of money to spend on a fancy vehicle when he could have done this in his old truck without worrying about what it was going to look like afterward. He was really and truly an idiot.

Mick parked in the lot, radioed his location to central dispatch, locked the Suburban, and set off half-running on the trail to the beach. A few pounds of excess flesh bulged over his belt but he could still move fast when he needed to. He was grateful that the Mercantile and the fire department had kept him active. He hadn't gained as much weight as most of the older men he knew. And he hadn't had a heart attack yet, or coronary bypass surgery, which had become something of a rite of passage for men his age.

The forest of tall trees and brush closed around him. He inhaled the ozone breath of the low, black clouds and tasted the moisture in the saturated air. A gathering electrical charge pulled at the hairs on his arms and back of his head. A few huge raindrops splashed off leaves and cratered into the sandy soil.

He stopped and peered into the dark brush beside the trail, listening for a repeat of the low growl he thought he had heard. Bear dung, still moist and full of undigested red berries lay in the mat of vines at the side of the trail. Sweat tricked under his T-shirt. The sound repeated, menacing, right in front of him. He turned stiffly to face it, wishing he hadn't left his radio in the Suburban.

Animal eyes glared behind the twin nose holes of a black snout. Snarling lips quivered over sharp white teeth. Mick relaxed a little. It was only Anna Davis's little black and white dog but its fierce, low growl suggested a much larger animal.

"Benny! Where's Anna?"

The dog backed up, still snarling. It turned its head briefly to look down the trail, swiveled its ears, and gave a sharp bark.

Mick moved to continue down the trail but the dog scrambled in front of him, barking incessantly. Benny was no more than eighteen inches tall, a long-haired terrier mix with fluffy white ears and a button nose. Even so, Mick was intimidated by the thought of Benny's sharp little teeth sinking into his leg.

The Turtle Lady appeared, calling to Benny to stand down.

"Oh, man, am I glad to see you!" she called out to Mick. She carried her backpack loaded with a tent and sleeping bag. "We've got to move fast." Breathing hard, she barreled past him.

Benny ran ahead on short legs, the hair on his ears and tail fanned out like a bottle brush.

"This storm, it's going to be bad," Mick huffed as he ran behind her.

"I know, I know. Can you feel it? We're going to get a lightning strike right about now."

"Oh hell," Mick muttered, turning on all the speed he could muster. He had never been close to a lightning strike before but the sense of impending violence was unmistakable. He could feel tingling in the soles of his feet.

Ten seconds later the air cracked with astounding sound and light, shaking the ground and showering the air with sparks. A hundred feet behind them the top half of a tall fir tree crashed, smoking, into the brush. A downdraft of cold air poured out of the black cloud above them followed by a deluge of hail.

Lightning exploded again and a tree fell over the path ahead of them. Anna and Mick scrambled over it and Benny scooted under. They slipped in the melting hail that had instantly turned the path into a stream. A strong gust of wind whirled over them, uprooting more trees. Emerging from the forest they could see trees all around the parking lot bending nearly double in the wind.

Anna ran to the front passenger door of the Suburban, head down to keep the hail from stinging her face, and swung out of her drenched backpack. Mick got his keys out of his pocket and aimed the key fob at the door, arm fully extended, as if the device were a weapon—or a magic wand. He pressed one of the buttons but didn't hear the usual chirping response from the car. Adjusting his glasses he studied the buttons on the device. After several weeks of new car ownership he was still confused about how it worked.

A cracking sound made him turn his head just in time to see a seventy-five-foot fir tree falling toward them in graceful slow motion. He grabbed Anna's arm and pulled. Wet, cold branches slapped his face and knocked him to the ground. As the tree slammed into it the Suburban jounced hard and commenced a hysterical horn blaring and blinking of headlights and taillights.

Mick scrambled out of the tangle of branches and saw that the trunk of the tree had landed on the top of the Suburban. Anna crawled out of a heap of thick, green boughs a couple feet away and kneeled on the pavement, lifting branches and calling for Benny. Blood trickled from a cut on her left forearm and her long, frizzy, white hair was pincushioned with fir needles and hail. A few small scratches cross-hatched her face. Benny clambered out from under the heap, muddy and wet, but wagging with obvious joy and relief at finding Anna. He gave her face a delicate lick and sniffed her injuries with evident concern and sympathy. She laughed and hugged him.

"Are you okay?" Mick shouted over the bleating of the car alarm, squatting to check her for serious injuries.

"Yes. Thanks. You saved my life." She smiled crookedly as she started to get up.

Mick prevented her from moving with a gentle hand on her shoulder. "Wait, we've got to see if you're all right first." He ran his hand over her head, parting the damp white hair to check for blood and bruises."

"I'm fine, really," she said. "Just this." She held up her bleeding arm.

Mick had too much experience with accident scenes to accept what a victim told him about her condition. The excitement and shock could mask all kinds of pain and serious injury. He tenderly probed around the cut on her arm, checking for broken bones. The cut wasn't deep and the bleeding had stopped.

"How are *you*?" Anna shouted over the din of the car alarm. "You're bleeding too." She pointed to his right ear.

He peered at his dim reflection in the car window and wiped at the blood oozing from a deep cut on the top of his ear. It didn't hurt yet.

"Okay, now let's get you up." Mick offered an arm as Anna hauled herself up to a standing position. She gave her arms and legs a shake and brushed fir needles off her clothes.

"Really, I'm okay," she said. The wind whipped her hair around her face. "At least the hail has stopped."

Mick tried to push the tree off the Suburban but it wouldn't budge. Anna went around and grabbed a branch to pull as Mick shoved but the heavy tree trunk had wedged itself into a deep dent in the roof above the front passenger door.

He shouted over the blaring alarm. "We're going to have to call and have somebody come get us." But the radio was locked in the car and he had lost the keys.

Thunder cracked above them and he heard another tree crash somewhere close in the woods. It was getting dark. The wind howled now, pelting them with projectiles that smarted like BBs, thunking chunks of bark and pine cones onto the steel body of the still honking Suburban. Trees shrieked, flailing their branches as if to ward off the attacking wind. The parking lot was deserted and the nearest phone, if it still worked, was a mile away. Though they would be sitting ducks if one of the bigger trees fell on the car, it would be safer inside.

It was beginning to look like they could be in serious trouble.

Anna dragged her backpack from under the tree branches as she shouted over the wind and the car alarm, "Come on, let's open the door!"

28

"The keys must be somewhere under here." Mick, on hands and knees, crawled as far as he could under the tree, searching in the near dark, cursing that his flashlight, too, was in the Suburban. After patting the ground blindly for a few minutes, unnerved by the increasing wind, he had to give up.

"Benny," Anna called. The dog came to attention, ears up, eyes ready. "Find the keys, Benny."

The dog tipped his head and whined. Clearly a question mark.

"Find Mick's keys, Benny." She pantomimed keys turning a lock and pointed at the tree branches.

Benny waded on short legs into the mass of green branches, poking his nose here and there. He barked sharply and dove into a thick layer of green. All of him but his tail disappeared into the pile momentarily then he leaped out with the keys between his teeth and delivered them to Anna.

"Good boy!" Anna shouted. She held the fob up and pressed buttons that silenced the infernal honking and released the locks with a chirp.

She went around and opened the driver's side door, boosted her pack into the back seat and climbed over the console into the passenger seat. Benny jumped in and stood on her lap, shivering.

Mick heaved himself into the driver's seat and let the wind slam the door shut. The relative quiet inside the car soothed his fear a little but his hand shook when he picked up the emergency band radio from the charger cradle and called dispatch.

"County dispatch, this is Cranberry Beach oh-two, do you read?" Mick said, holding the radio close to his face and consciously modulating his voice to the detached, laconic style customary in emergency services. He waited for a response, hearing only fragments of phrases broken by the intermittent fuzz of radio static.

"The storm's interfering with radio reception," he said to Anna who for the first time was beginning to look a little frightened.

"County dispatch, this is Cranberry Beach oh-two, do you read?" Mick said again into the radio.

A woman's voice answered through the crackling static. "This is dispatch, oh-two. Your transmission is breaking up."

"Dispatch, I and one other person are stuck in the parking lot at the state park. My vehicle is pinned under a fallen tree. Minor injuries. Request immediate assistance."

A long minute of faraway garble, then, "Oh-two, say again."

"Dispatch," Mick started to say, but he ducked, covering his head, when another tree crashed down on the Suburban. It slammed into the roof from the front, pushing a dent four inches into the cabin ceiling and shattering the windshield into a spider's web of cracks.

Mick's voice slid up in pitch. "Dispatch, for Christ's sake, we're in trouble out here at the state park."

" . . . read you, oh-two . . . get a unit out as soon as possible but . . ." A burst of static occluded part of the message. ". . . major emergency here . . ." Then nothing but a snowstorm of static.

"Jesus," Mick said, "I wonder what the hell's happening."

Two more trees fell. One landed heavily against the front driver's side door, the other crumpled the roof toward the back. A dense thatch of fir branches pressed in at every window, blocking out the last shreds of dusk.

"Give me the keys and I'll try the lights," Mick said.

He keyed the ignition to the accessory position and switched on the dome light which worked even though it was dislodged and dangling by its wires. The AM-FM radio spewed the same static as the emergency band radio, threaded occasionally with the wisps of Mexican mariachi music commonly heard in the area.

Anna leaned over the seat, got her cell phone out of her pack and tried it.

"No service," she said, zipping it back into its pocket.

Not surprising considering the violence of the weather.

"It's okay Benny," Anna said, caressing the dog's back. He panted like a miniature locomotive. Every inch of his body trembled.

Something big thumped onto the roof. Anna and Mick ducked and Benny dove for the floor, whining.

"You know," Anna said, turning in her seat to survey the damage with wide, wondering eyes, "This is a fairly sturdy car."

Mick shifted to get a look at the interior of the Suburban. The roof was crumpled in several places. A branch poked through one of the back cargo door windows. Jagged cracks crazed the windshield and there was a six-inch gap along the top where the glass had separated from its metal frame—but it hadn't collapsed.

"Yeah," he grinned. "It's new. Do you like it?"

"Yeah, nice color. How many trees do you think are on top of it?" A wobble in her voice betrayed her anxiety.

"Don't know—four or five?"

"How long do you think it'll be before they come and get us?" Anna asked.

"Hard to tell. Sounds like they're busy so it might be a while."

Actually their chances of being rescued before morning were probably nil. There would be fallen trees all along the road, a monumental task to chainsaw through them all, not to mention the downed power lines to deal with. And there would be higher priorities for emergency personnel than coming all the way out to the point for two people and a dog.

Mick could hear the wind howling despite the thick heap of boughs that blanketed them. Maybe they would be okay riding out the storm right here if all the trees had already come down that were going to fall on them.

"Well," Anna said. "We might as well get comfortable then." She reached over the seat to her backpack, pulled the water bottle out of its net pouch, moistened some Kleenex and dabbed at the blood around the cut on her arm.

"I've got a first aid kit in the back."

He tried to open the driver's side door. It was jammed tightly shut. He maneuvered himself between the two front bucket seats onto the back seat, then climbed over the back seat into the cargo area. He pried the lid off a heavy duty plastic storage bin, took out his EMT jump kit and passed it to Anna. Rummaging deeper in the bin through the collection of fishing gear, tools, and other flotsam, he located the bottle of hooch he kept for fishing. It was nearly a full fifth of Jameson's Irish Whiskey.

He tossed that into the back seat then wiggled forward into the driver's seat and opened the orange plastic jump kit with its orderly array of first aid supplies. Their future was uncertain but at least he could clean and bandage their wounds.

The cut on Anna's arm was about three inches long but only went through the top layers of her skin, brown and spotted from life in the outdoors. He irrigated bits of soil and fir needles out of the cut with sterile water and wiped away the remaining crusted blood. Anna seemed relaxed and interested in the procedure. She didn't flinch. Mick covered the cut with gauze squares and secured them with bandage wrapped round and round her arm.

Using the mirror on the back of the sun visor, he examined his own injury. A deep cut notched the upper curve of his ear. Thick, dark red blood oozed from it, pooling in the curved recesses of his outer ear, running in a sticky stream down his neck to the collar of his T-shirt.

"More mess than anything," he said, removing his glasses and dabbing at the blood with a dampened gauze pad. It stung when he touched the cut. And it probably needed stitches.

"Maybe I can do that," Anna said.

It was awkward craning his neck to look in the mirror as he worked on himself and impossible to see well enough to do the job without his glasses. He handed Anna the gauze pads and water and relaxed as she kneeled on the seat and leaned over the console to gently wash away the blood and debris.

It needed more than a Band-Aid to cover and protect the wound. Anna folded sterile gauze squares over the top of his ear, enfolded the entire ear in swaths of gauze, and taped it all over to hold it in place.

She sat back, surveyed her work, and laughed. "You remind me of a famous artist."

Mick's reflection in the mirror did bear a resemblance to Van Gogh's self portrait with bandaged ear. He put his glasses back on but they sat tilted up on the right because of the bulky wad of gauze. Anna grinned and glanced away with a giggle.

Mick checked the mirror again. He did look pretty damned funny. He turned to Anna and grinned. That sent her into gales of hysterical laughter. Benny pawed at her face, whining.

Mick thought he heard something on the scanner, picked it up and by habit held it close to his bandaged ear. This sent Anna into another round of belly laughs.

He switched to the other ear and tried hard to listen over her laughter. There was nothing but snow on the scanner. It was possible the main transmitting station at Spencer's Landing was knocked out.

"I'm sorry," she gasped. "Really, I didn't mean to laugh at you. It's just, you know . . . stressful." She wiped her eyes with her sleeve.

"No offense taken," Mick said. Wind buffeted the car from all directions, writhing the fir branches against the windows. "I've got to admit I'm stressed too. I've never been in a storm like this before."

"I have. Hurricane Isabel in North Carolina. It was like this, only more rain. The roof blew off of the house we were in."

Mick contemplated that as they soberly listened to the jet-engine sound of the wind. A storm strong enough to blow down the trees around them would surely be tearing roofs off buildings all over the peninsula. He should be out in it going house to house getting people evacuated. But he was stuck here, useless. His son, Sean would be safe in the big city of Portland and for that he was grateful. He hoped Bev had gone inland somewhere. And he hoped somebody had gotten out to the dune cottages to evacuate Amanda and her mom and the other people staying there. Actually, *he* should have stopped at the cottages before running out to the point. The official powers-that-be may not have gotten around to recognizing the fact, but it had been obvious by early this evening, to anybody with common sense who lived here and knew the place, that this storm was going to be a bad one.

The sound of the storm changed, jerking Mick back to alertness. In a minute he understood what had happened. Drenching rain had muffled the steel-edged sharpness of the wind's howl.

Water began to flow down the fir branches and trickle in rivulets over the cracked windshield.

"It's raining," Anna said. "It's raining *hard*."

Water sheeted down the windshield, diverting around the tree trunk resting against it, and through the gap where the top of the glass had sprung away from the frame. It flowed over the dash, into the radio, and splashed down over the console to flood the carpet.

Scooting back in the seat to edge his knees away from the drips, Mick grabbed the wet radio out of the charging cradle. Too late, it was soaked. He wondered how much worse it was going to get.

A blatting, musical tone like a tiny bugle call erupted inside the car.

"Oh, good lord, Benny." Anna collapsed in giggles again as a noxious cloud of dog fart diffused through the cab.

Benny raised his muzzle, laid back his ears and howled.

Mick pressed all the window switches but only one of the rear ones still worked. A gust of wet but fresh air barged in.

Benny stopped howling to fart again.

"Oh, Benny," Anna said, "You're scared too, aren't you." She held the trembling dog close, still giggling.

"Jesus H. Christ," Mick muttered as he reached over to pat around in the back seat for the bottle of whiskey.

Two inches of cold coffee dregs sloshed in the bottom of his travel mug. He tried again to open his window but it remained stuck shut. Oh, what the hell, he thought, and poured the coffee out on the floor. It left an expanding brown circle in the new and now marshy tan carpet. He poured a couple ounces of Jameson's into the cup and handed it to Anna.

She sipped the whiskey and murmured reassuring words into the fur of Benny's neck. The dog calmed down and the gagging vapors of his flatulence drifted out the window.

Mick took a big swig of whiskey from the bottle. He didn't usually drink his liquor straight, preferring to mix it with sugar and cream in hot coffee. It caused a burning spasm of his throat which quickly eased, leaving a warm, sweet, grassy taste. He took his glasses off and put them in the console. Tilted out of level by the bandage on his ear, the bifocals had made everything blurry.

"Are you Irish?"

Mick took another drink of whiskey, wondering why she would ask that.

"What?" he said after he had swallowed and the clutching throat reflex had subsided.

She pointed to the bottle.

"Oh," he said.

"And Mahoney's an Irish surname. And Mick's an Irish nickname," she said.

His great grandfather had immigrated to America with nothing but a single-minded desire to be American. Irish heritage had never been something of value in the family so the Mahoney name was the only Irish thing passed down through the generations.

"We're not really Irish," was all Mick said.

"Me neither," Anna said, sipping from the coffee cup. "But I do know the Irish word for whiskey."

She paused, but Mick didn't know quite what she expected from him. "So what's the word?" he asked.

"Usquebaugh. Translated from the old Irish, it means, literally, 'water of life.'"

Anna held her cup up to the stream of water that poured from the bent windshield, allowing the rainwater to dilute her whiskey.

"May you be in heaven before the devil knows you're dead." She raised the coffee cup in a toast to him, winked rakishly and drained it.

Mick refilled her cup and tipped the bottle for himself.

"Is there anything we can stuff in that opening to slow down the amount of water coming in?" Anna asked.

He crawled into the cargo area again and found a nylon windbreaker which he passed up to Anna. She stuffed it in the gap.

"That helps," she said. "But it's very wet up here. How's the back seat?"

"It's dry, come on back."

Anna boosted Benny over the console between the front seats and crawled over it herself. Mick went on hands and knees to the back of the cargo space to retrieve his bag of groceries. In the storage bin he found several candles and a plastic container of dry matches. He clambered back into the backseat and unloaded items from the grocery bag.

"We've got cheese and crackers and a can of ravioli."

"I've got apples and cashews in my pack—and a couple of forks."

Mick got his Swiss army knife out of his pocket, pleased that he would be able to use the can opener tool.

Anna lit candles and propped them here and there around the cab.

"It might be good to conserve the battery," Mick said as he leaned over the seat to switch off the overhead light and the ignition.

Anna nodded, "It's going to be a long night."

He checked his watch. Nearly ten o'clock.

"So Mick, tell me about yourself." Anna settled into the seat with a handful of crackers and some cheese.

Conversation. It *was* going to be a long night. But he liked Anna, she was different from the other women he knew, and she wasn't from Cranberry Beach.

"I'm not at all interesting," Mick said.

"We'll see about that."

3

An hour later Mick pushed the back cargo door open against the wind and the press of fir boughs. Benny sniffed and peered into the darkness but balked at jumping to the ground.

"Hey, I thought you had to go," Mick said to the dog.

"Wait—I'll help him. I have to go too." Anna crawled over the seat into the cargo area and backed out the door on hands and knees with Benny tucked under her arm. She pushed through the boughs until she was out of sight.

"There's a rain puddle," she called to him. "Ankle deep. I can't find any dry ground."

After a few minutes she reappeared at the door and boosted Benny in. The dog shook himself, flinging water all over the interior and Mick. Anna maneuvered around the springy mat of wet branches that kept trying to push the door shut and crawled in, soaking wet and giggling from the effects of the whiskey.

When she had clambered back to the seat, Mick worked his way out through the branches and directed his stream into the darkness. He was mildly buzzed himself by the whiskey, which was not a bad way to ride out a storm. They hadn't heard a tree fall for some time now so unless something else happened it seemed safe in the car. It would only be a matter of waiting until morning. There was nothing he could do until then. He just had to accept that the other people in the fire department would be out there in the community taking care of things.

He worked his way back to the seat where Anna sat peeling off her wet sneakers and socks. He took his off too and tossed them in the front seat.

"Okay," Anna said as she repositioned one of the candles. "Where were we?"

She had gotten him to talk nearly nonstop for the last hour, something he rarely did. But Anna knew how to ask questions to keep the conversation moving along. He had told her about his job at the Mercantile, the fire department, his house, a little about his ex-wife and their failed marriage. Anna made it easy to tell these things. And before he knew it, she might, pry up that other story that had lain, starved and cramped, under the floorboards like a fugitive for so many years. It was probably the sort of thing best left alone. He had always believed that. Until Sean got into trouble.

"Your turn," Mick said. "Time to tell about *you*."

"Okay." Anna combed through her hair with her fingers, anchoring it temporarily behind her ears. Fir needles poked out here and there, caught in the wiry white tangles. Deep wrinkles around her eyes and mouth were witness to a lifetime of sun exposure and smiling.

"I'm seventy-two years old. My husband passed away many years ago. I have one daughter, Megan, who lives in Dallas with her husband and my two wonderful grandchildren, William who is nine and Yolanda who is seven. I live most of the year in Newport, Oregon in a kind of condo with several friends and lately I've spent my summers out here on the peninsula."

"Looking for sea turtles—which can't live here."

She smiled and nodded. "That is the conventional wisdom, yes. They tend to inhabit warm, mostly tropical and subtropical waters. And Pacific Northwest coastal waters, though warmer in the last few years than ever before in recorded history, haven't reached subtropical temperatures. Until this summer. The water's getting very warm lately."

"From global warming." Mick added.

"Could be, but climate is something that changes slowly. It's impossible to say one or even a few hot summers in a row are the result of climate change. But we can say with certainty that this weather we're having right now is a big anomaly. It's seriously different from past patterns."

"And might have brought the turtles up here."

"Yeah. But nobody wants to listen to me. My papers have been rejected by the scientific journals and everybody laughs at me but I have reason to question the generally accepted facts of turtle ecology."

"And what reason is that?"

"Well, it's mostly in the metaphysical realm, so traditional scientists don't take it seriously. It comes from a dream."

"Uh . . ." This was beginning to sound a bit daffy to Mick. "You mean the kind of dream when you're asleep?"

"I was asleep when the image came to me. Though for some people visions like this can sometimes break through into waking consciousness."

Mick, skeptical but curious, said, "Go on. Tell the dream."

"Okay. It goes like this. There's a broad estuary bay to my left, bordered with green, forested hills. In front of me there's a little inlet of the bay and to the right, beyond a small spit of gravel and sand beach is the ocean. The earth under my feet is sandy. The air is warm with a delicious breeze. Trees and brush grow all around. It's a wild place. I see a blue houseboat in the water of the inlet. It has what seem like logs for pontoons but it isn't floating properly. One corner—the left rear as I look at it—is sinking. It has windows on either side of a door and a little chimney poking out of the slightly pitched roof. I say to a companion, "This is my home!" I feel a recognition, a rushing out of joy and welcome. It is so beautiful.

"Then I'm on the houseboat and the waves are very big. The houseboat is tossed about. I hang on tight. Then I'm in the water swimming. It's warm and I feel good. Blue waves break over me and the current tugs at my body. I feel the tide changing. A sea turtle swims near. I see she has something tangled around her head. It's a wad of plastic debris—fishing line and an old net float, a plastic bag. The sort of garbage that floats around in the ocean and never decomposes. I work it off with my fingers, feeling the leathery turtle skin. She's grateful for my help. She communicates this telepathically. There's more she wants to tell me but I can't understand what it is. Released from the knot of plastic garbage, the turtle swims toward the shore and I follow her. She crawls up the beach which takes a long, long time. She digs a hole in the dry sand on the upper beach, deposits her eggs and scrapes sand over them. Then she goes back into the water and swims away."

It was quiet for a minute while Mick gazed at one of the candles, thinking about the dream.

"How does that dream connect to you being on this particular peninsula?"

"Oh, I forgot to say. At the beginning of the dream I see the Cranberry Beach water storage tower across the inlet. It's a little confusing because the land forms in the dream don't match the peninsula very well. But the water tower was unmistakable."

The tall water tank, Mick recalled, was lettered with the name of the town.

"But aren't dreams supposed to be symbolic?" he asked. "Or something about your sex life? You're not supposed to take them literally, are you?"

"I think this dream is very symbolic. The houseboat, for example. It's like the turtle. A turtle's shell is her house that she carries on her back. Her *home*. In the dream the houseboat home, which I think of as a symbol for the whole ecology of the earth, is in danger of sinking, and soon it will be unlivable. Just like earth is becoming unlivable because of human exploitation. In the last two decades all species of sea turtles have become endangered and I don't think it's too much of a stretch to say this dream is about that."

"But what are you looking for out here? A turtle? Why not work on saving them where they actually live?"

"That's what's hard to explain. All I can say is that I believe we're sometimes called by our dreams to action on behalf of the soul of the world. My dream clearly told me the place is *here*.

"So I've continued my research regarding turtle habitat and I think it's possible they can adapt to a much wider range of conditions than most biologists give them credit for. As the environment gets hotter in their customary nesting sites, and food sources in tropical oceans dwindle, fewer offspring are able to survive. Populations are collapsing all over the world. To keep up with environmental changes, it would be natural for them to move north. Natural selection means those most able to adapt to changing conditions are the most likely to survive."

More environmental laws for the government to enact. Mick was beginning to get a little ticked off.

"Sea turtles are an ancient species that has adapted to lots of change over the eons. The challenge for them now is whether they can change fast enough to keep up with what's happening right now. They're facing a combination of human development and global warming that may be developing way faster than projected by the climate models."

Mick frowned.

"What's wrong?"

"So now we've got to save turtles along with salmon and owls and every little thing that lives in the mud. That bullshit only makes it harder for real people who have to make a living to survive."

"Oh." Anna nodded somberly. "I hear that a lot. Too many people whose livelihoods depend on the land end up getting the short end of the stick in some environmentally-related matter. What happened in Cranberry Beach?"

Mick sighed and tried to shake off the sarcasm that usually colored his comments on this subject. "You may have wondered why Cranberry Beach has no cranberries anymore."

"Pesticide bans?"

Mick nodded. "To protect the salmon runs, the EPA banned the pesticides we were using. That finished off the small farmers around here. Our economy was gutted. Nobody can afford to live out here anymore, even on land that's paid for. Got to pay taxes. Got to eat. No way to earn a good living. Now everybody just gets by any way they can."

"Isn't there an alternative to using pesticides in growing cranberries?"

"There are organic alternatives that don't affect the salmon the way the pesticides do, but it's way more expensive than using chemicals. There's some demand for organic berries in Seattle and Portland but it's not big, and there are only a few customers who will pay what it costs to grow them that way. Now the big east coast operations own just about the whole market. Around here it came down to salmon or cranberries and salmon won. We're just collateral damage."

"I know it's no comfort, but this kind of thing is happening all over the world. Sacrifices are being made to assure future generations will have a reasonable kind of world to live in."

"Why is it always the little guy who has to do all the sacrificing?"

Anna shook her head. "I don't know the answer to that. It's one reason I haven't ever considered myself an ardent environmentalist. Or pledged allegiance to any of the big political action organizations or marched with the zealots in the streets of Seattle. To me, most issues aren't as clear-cut as many of the idealistic activists see them."

"If they had to work for a living maybe they wouldn't have time to be so damned idealistic."

Anna raised an eyebrow. "To be fair, I think most of those idealistic young people would say that they *are* working—on something more important than just their own lives."

For a minute Mick felt chastised and ready to argue. But then he thought about Sean and the other young people who served with him as volunteers in the fire department. They would give their lives to save a neighbor. That was idealistic—but not so political.

After a minute Anna asked, "Is that why you're working at the Mercantile? You can't farm your cranberries?"

Mick's anger ebbed, taken over by sadness and regret. He looked away from Anna's intelligent, searching face. "My own cranberry bogs haven't been farmed for years. My dad did that but I never took it up after he passed away. I've worked at the Mercantile since I came back a long time ago.

"Came back from where?"

He took in breath to answer but let it out in a sigh and shook his head. "It's a long story."

"We've got time."

Mick held his wristwatch near a candle to check the time. "It's midnight," he said. "Only four and a half more hours until first light."

"I don't think I'm going to be able to sleep," she said. "This night is perfect for a really long story."

Several minutes of quiet passed. Mick thought Anna could be trusted with his secret and wouldn't judge him for it. But the habit of protecting it was too strong.

"Wait," Anna said, playfully holding her hands up in a time-out gesture. "I've got to pee again." She climbed over the backseat. "I can get the door—no problem. Don't say anything until I get back."

She unlatched the cargo door, pushed it open, turned around and backed out.

Mick heard her groan, "Holy shit."

"Got a problem?" he called out.

"Yeah. The water level's up about two feet from the last time I was out here."

After she returned, Mick crawled over the seat, found a flashlight in the storage bin and leaned out the back door with it. Foamy water churned nearly level with the Suburban's bumper. There was an ebb and flow to the water's movement that suggested the flood wasn't just an accumulation of rain water but an extension of the sea. The mat of branches surrounding them had muffled the sounds of the storm but with his head out the door he could clearly hear the surf crashing. It seemed to be nearly a quarter mile closer than it had been when they ran up the beach trail. The storm surge had started. And the ocean could very possibly wash right over this tip of the peninsula.

A creeping feeling of dread lurked in the back of his mind under the soft blanket of inebriation. The flashlight beam revealed nothing but the mass of dripping evergreen branches and crisscrossed trunks of slim Douglas firs. Luckily nothing really big had hit the Suburban. Maybe the frame hadn't buckled and left gaps where the rising water could gush in. There was no telling how high the water was going to get but Mick figured they were going to find out soon just how watertight a quality GM vehicle could be.

He closed the cargo door securely. Other than the hole in the back window where the branch had come through, the flashlight revealed no obvious gaps in the back door seals. There was no evidence of bent frames around any of the other doors either. But there was no assurance the water wouldn't push its way in through bolt holes under the carpet or a thousand other invisible cracks and holes.

"We should think about our options," Mick said, shining the flashlight out each window. "We're pretty much covered by trees but most of them are small. We could climb up through them and maybe make a run for it. There's higher ground about a thousand feet from here."

Anna, wide-eyed, shook her head. "I saw the storm surge from Hurricane Isabel. It was fast and powerful. If this one is anything like that we wouldn't be able to stay on our feet."

She was right. Mick could clearly hear the surf now, even inside the car. But he didn't like the idea of riding it out in something that could become more like a coffin than a boat.

"Maybe we should close the window then," Mick said, nodding toward their source of fresh air. "Better do it before the water gets high enough to short out the wiring in the window controls."

He clambered into the front seat, keyed the ignition and thought about leaving the window down an inch but decided against it. He closed it tight and climbed back over the seat.

"I've got some duct tape," he said, leaning over to dig around in the storage bin.

"Ah—the universal repair tool," Anna said, laughing.

Mick chuckled. "Not a chance in hell it'll really keep the water out but it's something to do."

When they were finished, silver tape outlined every door and window, bulging in great wads over the broken place at the top of the windshield and around the branch poking through the back window. Anna rubbed every inch of the tape with a spoon from her backpack to make sure it stuck to the upholstery and glass as tightly as possible.

Probably a futile exercise, Mick thought. Duct tape doesn't work well in wet conditions, but doing something eased the anxiety and claustrophobia.

"Are you religious?" he asked.

"Not in any formal way."

"Times like this, religion would be a comfort. But I never got into it."

Anna kneeled on the seat and angled the flashlight to shine out the window and down. "Can't see how high the water is," she said, switching it off.

Through the soles of his feet Mick could feel the current rolling under the floor.

"We could take a hint from Benny," Anna said, smiling.

The dog slept, curled up on the seat beside her, his nose twitching with some canine dream.

"At first he was frightened of the storm but now he's at peace," she said. "Maybe he doesn't know what danger he's in. Or maybe he just lives in the moment, in the here and now. And for now we're safe. And comfortable."

She stroked the dog's black and white coat and caressed his fluffy ears.

"He's wise in a way most of us humans aren't."

Ignorance is bliss, Mick thought gloomily.

They sat quietly for a time, listening to the wind and the surf and the contented snoring of the sleeping dog. Wax dripped from the candles propped in the cup holders, puddling on the upholstery and carpet. The candles were half gone now and probably wouldn't last the night.

"You saved my life and Benny's," Anna said. "I was going to try to get to the road and flag a car. With these trees coming down, we would never have made it. And then the water—that would have been the end for us. So thank you."

"No problem. All in a day's work." And this day isn't over yet, Mick said to himself.

"It must take a special kind of person to be a volunteer firefighter."

He heard that comment often. Some people just adored firefighters and thought volunteers were saintly and altruistic. And yes, it was an essentially altruistic thing when you came right down to it. But in Mick's opinion excessive admiration was undeserved.

"Naw." He shrugged. "What most people don't know is how much *fun* it is to do emergency work."

Anna raised her eyebrows, questioning.

"Really. You get to drive a big, noisy, orange firetruck. And any day can turn into an adventure of some sort. Putting out fires, rescuing people from the surf or from car wrecks or other predicaments they get into. I like that stuff. No two days are the same. And Bev, my boss at the Mercantile, never complains about me running off on an emergency call any time of the day. But what I like best is solving problems for people who are just about completely helpless in their situation. It makes you feel good, like you count for something in the community. It makes you feel like your life is worthwhile."

For most of the people in the department that was true. But for Mick it seemed that all the good he could ever do would never redeem the one wrong thing that had burdened nearly all his adult years.

Anna broke the silence, nudging his knee with her foot.

"And you save people's lives, that's got to be rewarding," she prompted, clearly trying to keep the conversation going.

"Yeah." He concealed the serious dismay he felt about their situation, speaking glibly, as if to a newspaper reporter. "Medical emergencies, especially, can be life-or-death situations. Sometimes

46

it's what you can do in the first few minutes of an emergency that makes all the difference in whether somebody makes it."

"There must be times when you risk your own life to help others."

"Not that many, really. Training and technology keep us safe in most situations."

The car shuddered as a wave rolled under them, bumping along from back to front. Anna grabbed for the arm rest. Benny lifted his head to look around sleepily, then lay down again, tucking his nose under his paw.

"Do you think we're going to make it through tonight?" she asked.

He thought about that as she gazed at him, her expression more wondering than fearful. Standard operating procedure in an emergency required him to take charge of the situation and reassure the victims, in this case himself as well as Anna and Benny. He had done what he could to prevent further harm but it had been pitifully inadequate. The ocean was in the beginning stages of rolling over them and he had no way of knowing how deep the water would run or how violent it would be. They could be tossed around like a drift log, battered and drowned as the car filled with water and no way to get out.

"To tell the truth," he said, "I don't know."

"These could be our last hours then."

Another wave rocked the car.

"Yeah," Mick said. There was a lump in his throat. Regret.

"Well then," Anna said, reaching for the whiskey. "How can we make the best of it?"

Now that mortality was staring him in the face, the secret he had boarded up inside himself was beginning to demand attention. A religious person could confess the bad things they had done and ask for God's forgiveness. But what if you weren't religious?

He put his hand out for the bottle after Anna had drunk from it. It was now or never. "I could tell you that long story."

The car lifted on a wave, floating. He could feel by the pressure on his back and legs that the Suburban was moving slowly sideways but remaining upright.

Anna closed her eyes and relaxed back into the seat. "Good," she said. "Let's hear it."

He struggled to push the words through the tightness in his throat. "I haven't lived an honorable life." Seconds passed as he reeled from the visceral effect of that statement.

Anna glanced at him. "I'm listening."

He gazed into the blackness beyond the windows and started to speak but the words choked off. He shook his head and shrugged.

"Where was it you came back from? The place you mentioned before, when you went to work at the Mercantile."

"Long Beach."

Anna prompted again. "California?"

"Yeah. I was in the Navy."

"Oh yeah? When?"

"1968. Right out of high school. I had a bad draft number, signed up with the Navy to avoid being drafted into the Army."

"No shame in that. A lot of guys did it."

"No, there wasn't a problem with that. My dad had been in the Navy in World War II. I thought he would like it that I signed up. And I think he did, kind of. But he never talked about it. Never talked about anything. The only thing he said when I left for basic training was that war wasn't anything to glorify and that I should do my best at whatever I got assigned to and come back in one piece."

"Which you did," Anna said, looking Mick over. "You seem to have all your arms and legs and things."

"Actually, I screwed up big time."

A wave slid up over the window behind Anna and washed back down. Mick could feel water oozing up from below the carpet, cold on his bare feet. He shifted and pulled them up onto the seat, trying to ignore the floaty sensation of sideways movement and the slight vertigo it brought on.

Crossing his arms over his chest, he gazed at a spot on the ceiling. A window of memory opened like a movie.

48

"I was assigned to a guided missile frigate in port in Long Beach. This was in the fall of 1969. I was only a grunt. Always painting things, not much else. We were supposed to ship out for Subic Bay, the Philippines, as soon as some repairs were made. But some freaks on the crew were sabotaging the ship. Doing anything to delay shipping out. Things got broken, parts went missing. Important, expensive stuff fell into the bay. The day before we were supposed to leave port there was a fire in the engine room. Burned a lot of wiring that had to be replaced, which took months.

"So the ship had gotten the attention of the powers that be. It was being watched. But everybody was crazy during that time. The whole Vietnam war was crazy."

"I know," Anna said.

"A lot of guys were doing drugs, including about half the ship's officers. Mostly marijuana and hash but there was some heroin too and a lot of LSD. People were stoned all the time. It was a big part of the military culture in that era. Maybe because it was such a stupid, hopeless, pointless war."

"Were you into drugs too?"

"Nah. I was a small-town boy. We never had that stuff in Cranberry Beach when I was in high school. Not like it is now. I was naïve and generally not interested.

"But I had some friends on the ship who liked marijuana. And one boring, endless day I let them take me into an equipment compartment and teach me how to smoke a joint."

The car wallowed as a wave washed over them and sheeted down the windows. The mat of tree branches seemed to be absorbing most of the wave energy and holding the Suburban upright. Though several trees had fallen across it, they clearly weren't heavy enough to hold it down in the rising water. The ocean seemed to be lifting the trees and the car together. Mick stopped talking to check the door and window seals.

"We're floating like a boat," he said. "And still pretty much water tight."

Anna, her feet now tucked under her on the seat, pointed to the inch of water sloshing around on the floor.

"Well, at least it's not coming in very fast," Mick said.

Another wave pushed them abruptly sideways. Water trickled through the wad of tape on the broken windshield.

"All will be well," Anna murmured. "All will be well, all manner of things will be well." She continued to chant what sounded like a prayer for a few minutes, her body relaxed, her eyes closed. She breathed deeply in and out then turned her head to look at him.

"So you smoked your first joint and that's when the ship got busted."

"How did you know that?"

"I was in Long Beach then. A nurse at the VA hospital. We heard that about three-quarters of the officers and enlisted men serving on the James Lee Ericson were arrested, did time in the brig and dishonorably discharged."

"Not everybody went to the brig. Some of us were just discharged—dishonorably—and sent home."

"That's not such a bad thing. Everybody makes mistakes or gets in a jam sometime. I'm surprised it's still such a big deal for you."

"Getting kicked out of the Navy was damned humiliating but that isn't the whole story. See, when I got home everybody was so happy to see me. And you remember how, in those days, in some places anyway, the guys would come home and people didn't respect them. There was so much opposition to the war and people can be so simple minded. They turned their anger and disapproval onto the innocent young men who had gotten dragged into the service. A lot of guys wouldn't even wear their uniforms in public.

"The folks in Cranberry Beach wanted to make the point that they were *proud* of their veterans. Sixteen boys from my high school had gone into the service. Six died and nine went other places to live after they were discharged. So I was the only one to actually come home. If I had known they were going to go nuts like that I wouldn't have come back right then. But they made a parade for me, drove me through town in the back of a pickup, yelling and cheering and waving American flags. I meant to tell them the truth but there just wasn't a good time on that first day home.

50

"My dad was enjoying being a big shot, with everybody congratulating him and all. And the mayor made a speech saying what a fine person I was and how the whole community was so proud of me. Nobody asked why I was back home after only two years in the Navy.

"So the next day I tried to tell my dad the real story but he wouldn't listen. I told him I'd had some trouble but he waved that away. Said it was natural for a Navy man to get his dukes up in a barroom fight or something like that. Said he didn't want to hear about it, that it was over and done and life was starting over for me now. I never got it out that the discharge was dishonorable.

"And the other thing was—my dad thought smoking dope was just about the most depraved thing a person could do. Most of the people around here felt the same way. Back then people thought that marijuana was no different than injected heroin.

"I got the job at the Mercantile right away. Bev and Merle were thrilled to have me work for them and except for one time I never even looked for another job. Never wanted to fill out a job application where I had to give details about my military service. I never told anyone the truth until this minute."

"Not your wife?"

"Nope." Mick was miserable. "And the people of Cranberry Beach still call me their Vietnam vet. Though I told them I never went to Vietnam and all I ever did was paint. It didn't matter to them. I never had the courage to make them listen."

The gently bobbing car was quiet for a while as Mick straightened and rearranged the candles. Two of them had burned out already and the others were getting short.

"These are all the candles I've got," he said. "But we can use the flashlight if we need to."

"It'll be okay. Morning will come." Anna sat with her eyes closed, absently caressing the sleeping dog.

"You've waited a long time to tell this story," she said.

"It wasn't that bad. I thought I could live with it."

"Just talking about it is a step toward healing. Did you say your dad had passed away?"

"Yeah. Mom too."

"Who else do you want to tell?"

"Sean." Mick's voice caught and trembled. Tears watered his eyes. "I should have told Sean a long time ago. That was something he needed to know and I didn't tell him."

"Why did he need to know it?"

"He got busted for marijuana too, eighteen months ago. Maybe he wouldn't have gotten into it if he had known what happened to his old man."

"I don't know Mick. Now that it's legal, I don't know if there's any way to keep the kids from using it."

"And I didn't tell him when he was in jail either or after he got out. He doesn't know what a chickenshit sonofabitch I am. He just keeps telling me how damned sorry he is to have disappointed me and his mom."

Another candle guttered out in a pool of molten wax. Mick brushed tears from his cheeks.

"In my opinion," Anna said, "Smoking marijuana isn't a big enough crime to be put in jail for. The drug laws in this country are medieval."

"He had enough of it on him that night that it automatically qualified as a felony. Intent to sell. And it was true, he was selling it to kids who weren't old enough to buy it legally. He said he could make more money selling marijuana to friends at one party than he could bussing tables at the Crow's Nest for a month. He thought he could trust his friends and that it would be safe. But somebody blabbed."

Tears stung Mick's eyes and made his voice quaver. "The county prosecutor wanted to make a point in light of the new marijuana legislation so he recommended the maximum sentence. Sean spent six months in jail and now he's a convicted felon. Maybe I could have prevented that if I had been honest with him."

Mick sobbed with his hands covering his face. Never before in his adult life had he allowed himself to cry like this, in front of another person. But now it felt right, like something he had needed to do for a long time.

Two more candles snuffed out in wisps of sweet-smelling smoke. Anna picked up the whiskey bottle, took a drink and offered it to Mick. It was almost empty.

"Finish it," she said.

He wiped the tears off his face then tipped the bottle up and drained it. The car dipped and wallowed as Anna shifted her position to get more comfortable. She picked Benny up and put him on her lap then stretched her legs out and tucked her feet between Mick's hip and the back of the car seat. He stretched his legs out on the seat beside her. The last candle flame winked out and darkness enfolded them.

"Do you want the flashlight on?" he asked.

"No, let's save the battery. This is okay."

The glowing green circle of his watch showed two more hours until first light. In the dark he could hear water trickling somewhere and the wash of waves in the fir boughs.

Muzzy with tears and whiskey, Mick relaxed and drifted toward sleep but in a few minutes jerked awake.

"Damn."

Anna's body tensed and Benny gave a muffled woof and growl.

"What is it?"

"I didn't close the shutters on the house."

"Oh." She relaxed. "Will it be all right, do you think?"

"I don't know—there'll be a lot of water on the floors if the windows break. Hardwood floors, my grandfather put them in."

He shifted into a more comfortable position, fell asleep lulled by the rocking of the waves and dreamed that the old maple tree crashed down on the roof of his house. His grandfather came with a chainsaw and said nothing was ever so broken it couldn't be fixed.

* * *

It was well past midnight but Amanda was still up, thumbing the TV remote, inching the volume up a little more, to hear over the howling wind and pounding surf outside. She knew that her mother, asleep in the bedroom with an empty wine bottle on the floor beside her, wouldn't complain that the TV was too loud. Cross-legged on the couch with a super-sized bag of popcorn, a two-liter bottle of Coke, and a box of chocolate donuts, Amanda watched a movie meant for much older viewers.

"No, Joey," she said, pushing at her big black dog who had jumped onto the couch. "Get down."

He trembled and leaned against her, panting and trying to crawl into her lap. His ears swiveled at the sounds of things tumbling across the roof.

"Look, you stupid thing, you've spilled the popcorn. And get your stupid wet feet off me."

She brushed popcorn off the couch and didn't notice that it floated across the floor on several inches of foamy water.

An emergency message interrupted the movie. "It's just a test," Amanda said. She flipped channels several times before she found one without the message.

"Cartoons, Joey." She offered the dog a chocolate donut which he refused.

He raised his head and howled a duet with a far-away siren.

"Oh for Christ's sake, cut that out." She tried to push him off the couch but he gripped the edge of it with his claws and leaned all his weight against her.

Something big crashed into the cottage. There was a sound of breaking glass. Amanda's mother stumbled out of the bedroom rubbing her eyes and blinking. She stared at the floor with a funny, stupid look on her face. Amanda stood up on the couch to see what she was looking at. Swirling foamy water covered her mother's feet.

The lights blinked off then on again as her mother lunged into the living room and scooped Amanda up. The first wave hit before they reached the door.

4

Mick woke to dim light and an aching back. The car wasn't floating anymore. He could see Anna still asleep with her white hair fanned across the seat back, her bandaged arm across her chest. Benny, awake in her lap, swiveled his ears to listen to the sound of birds crying over the now distant sound of the surf. The storm had ended and morning had come, confirmed by a few amber beads of dawn light falling through the mat of fir branches around the Suburban.

The whiskey bottle lay empty on the soggy carpet but his head was surprisingly clear of hangover. Wonderfully clear. He felt better than he had in years. It had been a relief to tell Anna about the secret that had burdened him for so long. At some point he would have to tell Sean and Bev and his old friend Wally, which wouldn't be easy. But he had made a good start last night.

Something bonked onto the roof of the Suburban and made a bouncing roll off the side. Bird feet pattered around above them and a crow squawked.

Anna stirred, stretched her arms and pushed Benny off her legs.

"So much for sleeping in," Mick said.

Something else bounced on the roof followed by the brassy caw of the crow. Benny glared at the ceiling and gave a sharp bark.

"Crow's trying to break open a clam," she said, yawning. She smoothed her hair back with her hands and rubbed her eyes. "The top of the car must not be completely covered with trees."

Mick rearranged his tingling limbs.

Anna smiled at him. "We came through it."

He grinned as he glanced around to survey the broken windows, the dented roof, the upholstery sooted and streaked with candle wax. Everything under the hood was probably waterlogged, a total loss. He suspected it wasn't fully insured.

He reached over the front seat to pick up the radio handset. It was dead. Water dribbled out of it when he turned it over.

Anna tried her cell phone but it was still out of service.

"I need to get back to town," Mick said. "There's got to be a lot of damage. Jeez, I hope everyone's all right." He retrieved his damp and sandy shoes and socks.

Another clam smacked onto the roof, this time with a wet, splatting sound. With a braying whoop the crow thudded onto the roof and stabbed away at the food with its beak.

Benny hopped over the seat and went to the back doors. Scratching at the duct tape, he whined and pressed his nose to the crack between the doors.

"Wait a minute, I've got to get my good shoes on," Anna said to Benny as she dug in her pack.

Mick crawled into the cargo area, pulled tape off the doors, wadded it into a sticky ball and pushed the door open far enough to let Benny jump out.

"The water's gone," he called out.

He gratefully breathed the fir-scented air as he forced the door open against the thicket of branches and pushed through it to the topmost layer. The smell of the sea and beach washed over him on a warm, buoyant wind.

Trying to focus without his glasses, it took some time to grasp what he was seeing. It was like an old science fiction movie where survivors crawl out of their bomb shelters and everything has been transformed to gray, dusty rubble. But here it wasn't dust and ashes, it was wet sand covering everything as far as he could see--which wasn't far.

"Anna—could you reach my glasses in the console?"

She crawled back to the front seat, retrieved them, and handed them up to him.

The scene was still blurry, inconceivable. He pulled part of the bandage off his ear and repositioned the glasses so they sat straight. But even with corrected vision, the landscape before him bore no resemblance to the one he last saw yesterday.

No trees remained standing in the park. He turned to look for the rising sun. It floated like an orange balloon in a clear blue sky just above the horizon. The hills beneath it, far away on the eastern shore of the bay, were a solid and familiar reference point. But looking south he saw only mounds of gray-coated sticks where a forest of tall fir trees had stood.

Anna, in dry socks and hiking boots, climbed to the top of the Suburban and turned to scan in all directions.

"I don't know how we survived this," she said. She reached to pick up an oyster caught in the crook of a branch.

"This came from the bay. There are oysters and clams all over the trees. The storm surge must have filled the bay and then washed back out over this area. So we got it from two directions last night."

"Jesus. I'm glad we didn't try to run for higher ground. How high do you think the surge was?"

Anna shaded her eyes with a hand. "There's nothing left standing that would show a high water line. But to get all these oysters over this far it had to have been a big volume of water with scouring waves."

Heaps of downed trees covered the ground as far as Mick could see. Their interwoven branches had held the Suburban in an upright position and had added their buoyancy to the heavy vehicle.

"These downed trees all around us helped keep us afloat, like a giant raft," he said, "and kept us from tipping over."

It would have been easy—and probably fatal—for water to gush through the holes in the windshield and the broken back door window if the Suburban had tipped.

"Do you think the worst of the flooding was out here at the point?" Mick asked.

"No way to know until we get back."

"We can walk down the beach to town," he said. Only take us—what—a couple hours? After we get over these mounds of trees, the beach looks clear."

Benny lifted his head to sniff at the sky, rotating his ears like radar dishes.

"Listen," Anna said. "Benny hears something."

Mick heard the faint wumpa-wumpa of a distant helicopter. The sound grew quickly, coming from the south directly toward them.

"Are we going to get rescued already?" Anna asked.

Mick shook his head. "Doesn't sound like the Coast Guard."

In a few seconds the red and white helicopter passed over them and angled off over the bay to the north.

"MedEvac," Mick said. "Serious injuries. Looks like they might be taking someone to Seattle, to the Harborview Trauma Center."

Two minutes later a second MedEvac chopper passed over them, also headed north.

"This worries me," he said. "We've got to get going."

"Is that another helicopter?" Anna asked, shading her eyes and pointing to a speck in the sky to the southwest.

"Yeah." The sound of that one was faint but familiar. "That's a Coast Guard chopper. And it looks like there's more than one. Something's going on down near Cranberry Beach."

* * *

They picked their way around piles of trees and pools of seawater to the packed sand of the deserted beach and hiked south toward the town. Anna, in hat and sunglasses, carried her fully loaded pack while Benny zigzagged the beach ahead of them. Mick, lugging the EMT jump kit, struggled a little to keep up, his feet blistering from the damp socks. The weather was balmy and still but the surf remained high and eerie piles of shredded debris bore witness to the violence of the storm that had passed through only a few hours before.

When they got closer to town, Mick could see with the binoculars that a major operation was underway.

"Two Coast Guard helicopters are dropping rescue swimmers and baskets," he said, pointing to the near shore. "And there's TV coverage." He nodded toward a swarm of small helicopters buzzing around above the town, well out of the way of the big Coast Guard choppers.

As they walked south the nature of the debris tangled all along the beach told a grim story. Pink tufts of wall insulation sprawled across the sand, tangled with seaweed and umbrellas, potted plants, yellow pajamas, tree branches, a car seat, some picket fencing, and canned vegetables from someone's pantry. Along the shore the few trees left standing were bent and twisted. None of the houses they saw had roofs.

"I hope to hell everybody got out." He pointed to one of the wrecked houses. "These folks, the Tilsons. I saw them leaving when I came out to get you."

Benny barked and scratched at something buried in the sand.

"Mick. Wait a minute." Anna knelt to brush wet sand away from a mound of soggy, gray fur. It was a house cat with a jeweled collar. She stood and gazed in the direction of the town. With a worried frown she said, "This is not a good sign."

Benny crisscrossed in front of them, sniffing and pawing at the increasing litter of storm debris. A jumble of splintered boards, window casings and plastic gutters jammed up against the high waterline of white driftwood logs.

"Unbelievable," Mick said, shading his eyes to look south. "The water tower's still standing. But the cellular tower and emergency services antenna are gone."

The Coast Guard helicopters hovered out beyond the surf line with a motor lifeboat bounding over the waves below them. He could tell that the storm had changed the beach near the town but it was too far away to see it clearly.

A quarter mile down the beach a raucous mob of gulls and crows rioted in the driftwood. Judging by their exuberance, they were feeding on something big. He felt a pang of dread. Several other gangs of carrion-eating birds brawled here and there along the beach, more flying in from all directions.

"We'd better take a look," he said.

They found the dog first, still relatively intact because of his thick black fur. The same wasn't true for the little girl.

Mick batted the frenzied birds away with a stick. They had feasted on the soft flesh of the face and eyes. A butterfly clip dangled from the long, dark hair and foul smelling sand drifted over the bare arms and torn red dress. Sand fleas gnawed in the pecked places.

"Amanda." Mick dropped to his knees beside the child. "I should have . . ." Nausea wrenched at his stomach. "If I had only gone out to warn them . . ."

Crows took turns swooping, screeching, and wheeling out of reach to circle back again. Benny barked and leaped at them. With outstretched claws they knocked Mick's cap off. On his knees he swung at them again and again with the stick, cursing them.

"You can't keep them off her that way," Anna shouted over the din.

"This isn't right." Emotion clenched at his throat. "They can't just chew on her this way."

He stood up and with both hands on the stick swung hard and connected with one of the big black birds, sending it tumbling onto the sand. The others retreated, lighting on the driftwood to curse back at him.

"Why weren't they evacuated?" Mick stared at Anna, his mind struggling with the question. "There had to have been time. Why didn't anyone go out there?"

"Maybe that's something you can find out in town. Which is probably where you need to be right now." She picked up his cap and handed it to him. "Amanda can't be helped. But maybe there are others who need you."

He brushed sand off his cap, put it back on and kneeled again beside Amanda. He untangled the butterfly clip from her hair and put it in his pocket. Then he retrieved a damp slip of paper from the sandy pocket of the red dress.

60

"You might be interested in this."

The pencil drawing was faint but still legible, richly detailed with anatomical observations including a perfect rendition of a partially severed neck.

"She told me yesterday that she had found one of these on the beach."

Anna studied it briefly, nodded, folded the paper carefully and slipped it into the back pocket of her jeans.

"Let's see if we can cover her body to slow down the predation," she said.

They covered Amanda with a twisted remnant of corrugated metal roofing held in place with several big pieces of driftwood. Anna marked the site with a boot stuck on the end of a long stick jammed into the sand. She took off her sunglasses to wipe away tears.

Mick watched the crows fly off to investigate other venues farther down the beach. "Amanda's mother is probably somewhere around here," he said.

"We could look for her, try to protect her body too."

"Do you think there's any chance she's still alive?"

Anna shook her head. "No. I think the odds are probably against that."

"Okay. Let's go. Let's get back to town. We're almost there."

The change in the shoreline became more and more apparent as they approached the town. The beach, instead of continuing in a more or less straight line due south, now curved sharply to the east. They rounded the curve and looked across a wide inlet of choppy sea water. The town of Cranberry Beach, or a greatly revised version of it, lay on the other side of the water.

It was beyond comprehension.

"The storm surge," Anna said, "It must have broken right through the peninsula. It made this part an island."

Mick, bewildered, stared at the wide channel of water connecting the ocean and the bay. "The highway's gone," he said. "And where's my house?"

He turned to face Cranberry Beach. "The Mercantile. Thank God, it's still standing. But the sewage treatment plant is gone." He swung around, reaching with his arms for absent landmarks.

"And the dune cottages were there . . . and my house would have been right about there."

He pointed to the middle of the channel where everything he had owned was supposed to be. It was unreal, like turning to the wrong page of a book and landing in the middle of a different tale altogether. It seemed like he should be able to flip back and get to the right page, back to his own familiar story.

They walked toward the broken area of overhanging grassy sod at the edge of the newly formed beach. The remains of the amputated county road lay scattered in chunks of asphalt. Strands of barbed wire fell away from an interrupted row of fence posts and disappeared into the sand.

"Here's my north pasture," Mick said. "I helped my dad put up the barbed wire when I was in the eighth grade." He was silent for a long time as his gaze swept across the transformed land.

"Dad raised a few steers. But the good kind of grass never grew very well here. Sandy soil. He had to buy hay for them . . ."

"Mick," Anna circled her arm around his shoulders and gently turned him away. "This is a huge loss. It's going to take some time to absorb it."

She pointed across the water. "But right now you're needed over there. Look, there's a fire truck and people working over there. We should try to get their attention. They can send someone over in a boat for us."

He squinted and shaded his eyes to watch the activity on the far shore. Anna unzipped a pocket of her backpack, pulled out her binoculars and handed them to him.

"Jesus. They're extricating someone from an RV that's partly sunk in the sand. I think I see more RVs turned on their sides. Some are buried and halfway into the water. Christ almighty. The storm surge must have gone right through the Golden Sands."

He scanned the opposite shore to the east where the RV park had been, then back across the channel and along the eastern stretch of the newly created island they were standing on.

"What the hell . . ." He saw the angular orange roof of a truck several hundred feet down the beach, jutting up under a jagged pile of trees and broken building materials. A metal bracket holding an array of emergency lights straddled the roof.

He handed the binoculars to Anna and took off running toward it carrying the EMT kit.

The crushed and mangled rescue truck had clearly rolled repeatedly. Mick, breathless from running, dragged boards and branches away from the driver's side door and wrenched at the handle. The twisted metal wouldn't budge. Two men occupied the inside of the cab, seatbelts in place across their chests. They wore helmets with their names stenciled on the sides: Tenney and Whittaker. Deep lacerations shredded their faces and necks.

Mick boosted himself up onto the hood and leaned in through the missing windshield. He reached below the collars of their turnout coats to feel for carotid pulses. Nothing. The eyes of the two men were open and fixed on some faraway scene, as if daydreaming.

Sand filled the cab up to the level of the steering wheel. The color of their skin was like the sand. A deep, ragged wound, washed clean of blood, ran between Tenney's jaw and shoulder.

He heard Anna's whisper. "Oh, my God, Mick."

"What the hell happened?" He couldn't take it in, couldn't make any sense of it.

Anna leaned in through the passenger side window to look closely at Tenney's wound.

"What's this?" She pulled something from the wound. A round, black thing. A rock. She moved around to the driver's side.

"Mick, you've got to take a look at this." She pointed at the lower part of the door.

He climbed down off the hood and looked where she was pointing. "Oh Jesus. I don't know. It's just all wrecked. The storm." He was mentally foggy, unable to focus.

Anna dragged some pieces of wood away and crawled under the truck to take a closer look. Reaching up into the area where the cab joined the steel frame, she brought out another black rock, fist-sized.

"This is asphalt. From the road." She held it up for Mick to see.

He swept his arm, indicating hundreds of similar black chunks strewn all over the beach.

"So?"

"Hmmm." She studied the object in her hand then dropped it on the sand with the others like it. "I guess it could have gotten up there when the truck rolled in the water."

She examined a fan-like pattern of scratches and holes in the orange paint of the driver's side door.

"But something's not right here."

A lot wasn't right. For Mick the novocaine effect of shock was beginning to wear off, allowing reality to sink in. The two men in the truck—his friends—were dead. Amanda too. And her mother and her dog. His land, his house—disappeared off the face of the earth. Along with half of Cranberry Beach. He sat down on a log and covered his face with his hands to shut it all out.

"They're coming," Anna said in a few minutes. The sound of two jet skis speeding toward them from the other side reminded him there was work to do. He picked up the jump kit and walked with Anna and Benny to the edge of the water.

"Hey, Mick," one of the teenaged boys called out as soon as they beached the jet skis, "Oakley said to get you over there ASAP. A lot of people are stuck in RVs on the beach and the tide's coming up."

Mick glanced back at the rescue truck. It was probably above the high tide line. Tenney and Whittaker could wait for recovery operations. Survivors needed help now.

He turned to Anna, to help her board the jet ski. But, with Benny trotting along beside her, she had walked away toward the east, shading her eyes to look at something on the water.

"Anna!" he shouted. "Come on. We've got to go!"

She turned and gestured that he should go and leave her. "I'm fine. Really!"

He handed the jump kit to one of the boys and jogged over to where Anna stood looking at something floating in the channel.

"I can't come with you right now," she said. "It's absolutely necessary that I stay here. For a while anyway."

Mick followed her gaze to a little structure bobbing in the choppy water. It looked like a tiny house, painted a bright sky blue, with a bent stovepipe chimney poking up through the shingled shed roof. It was a fishing shack, broken loose from an inland river bank, barely afloat on a chunk of white Styrofoam.

"Sometimes the dream world intersects with what most of us call the real world," she said. "That's happening now. It's here—my dream. The channel, the water tower. And there's the blue houseboat. And this." She took Amanda's drawing from her pocket.

Mick looked again at the fishing shack. "That's not exactly a houseboat."

"It's not precisely what I remember from the dream. But it's close enough."

"You're not going to swim out to it are you? The current looks dangerous."

"I don't need to do that. It's usually best not to take things too literally in spiritual matters. I just need to be here, to wait."

"For what?"

She smiled, held her hands out, empty of explanation, and shrugged.

"I don't know."

Two weeks after the storm Mick sat alone in the Olympia offices of Puget Sound Fidelity. He had been waiting nearly a half hour while Bob Evans, the loan officer handling his mortgage, consulted a supervisor. The devastating storm, compared by experts to that of an east coast hurricane, qualified victims for FEMA assistance. But Bob had explained that the low-interest government loans offered by that program to private citizens were for rebuilding, not for covering existing mortgages.

Bob had flipped through documents in the file folder bearing Mick's name, nodded his head and mumbled occasional "uh-huhs" as Mick described the damage to his property. The loan officer had glanced briefly at the photos and newspaper clippings Mick had brought and passed them back saying they weren't needed for the file.

Now Mick sat absently rubbing his damaged ear. He hadn't taken time to get medical attention for it after the storm and the wound had healed without closing up, leaving a deep notch that itched sometimes.

He shuffled through the photos and clippings, wondering how his life could have changed so abruptly. But at least he was alive. Twenty-three had perished. Amanda, her mother and another couple from the beach cottages. Tenney and Whittaker who had been on their way to evacuate the cottages when the storm surge hit. And seventeen from the RVs that had washed into the sea.

The deputies sent to evacuate the RV park that night hadn't been able to maneuver through the chaos of southbound traffic that clogged both lanes heading out of Cranberry Beach. The sheriff, faced with a panicky press of tourists and residents, had finally given the order to evacuate by all means possible including using the northbound lane of the highway. The deputies had gone on foot toward the Golden Sands, battered by wind, rain and appallingly close surf. They hadn't made it in time.

The water in the bay had risen, silently flooding Mick's cranberry bogs and oozing over to the RV park. It had risen under the RVs without anyone noticing. Lightning shorted out telephone wires and knocked the cellular tower out of commission but remarkably, electrical power and cable TV remained on until just before the catastrophic breach. Many of the people who decided to ride out the storm in their RVs had been cozily watching movies until it was too late to leave. Some had been asleep. When the warning finally flashed across their TV screens the water outside their doors was already thigh deep and flowing hard. Those who went out to spread the alarm among their neighbors were quickly swept away and drowned. The ones who remained inside clung to anything they could grab onto as the huge vehicles rolled over and over, pushed into the bay by a wall of churning, muddy water. That was at high tide. When the tide shifted, all the water now stuffed into the bay turned around and rushed out through the new channel, tumbling the RVs toward the ocean like boulders in a mountain stream.

Why the bay chose the RV park and Mick's land as its new exit channel was still a much-debated topic of TV interviews and newspaper reports. Mick thumbed through the articles he had collected. There was disagreement on details, but most experts agreed that the destruction had occurred on two fronts.

The storm's extremely low atmospheric pressure caused the surface of the ocean to bulge, making the water many feet higher than usual. Forty-foot waves rode the bulge on a high tide that coincided with the storm's landfall. The storm surge had pushed in from the ocean, smashed the dune cottages, and followed the path of least resistance along Decker Creek to the road. There the surf had plowed through the raised asphalt roadbed where Rutter Road intersected with the highway, breaking it and opening up a passage for ocean waves to rush toward the bay.

At the same time, ten inches of rain and hail gushed onto the eastern hills in two hours and all of that had drained into the bay via its three rivers. The navigation channel which normally emptied the bay at the north point of the peninsula was incapable of handling the enormous volume of backed up water. It had to go somewhere.

One of the newspaper clippings featured a topographic profile. It showed how Rutter Road, running all the way from the bay on the east to the dune cottages on the west, had been constructed by cutting through the central north-south ridge of old dunes. This had been done in the early 1900s for cranberry transportation. It was this spine of ancient, forested dunes that had, for thousands of years, made the peninsula so solid and impervious to the sea. Most of the highway was built along the spine. But Rutter Road, where it intersected with the highway, lay a mere six and a half feet above sea level. And only a few feet to the west of the highway, the tidal marsh dipped immediately to sea level and the inlet of Decker Creek. Mick's house had stood a few hundred feet to the northeast of this low-lying intersection. But never before in his own memory or in stories he had heard from his father or grandfather had the sea come up Decker Creek as far as the road.

He held up an aerial photo taken a couple days after the storm. The new channel and its borders of littered beach spanned about three-quarters of a mile from the middle of his north pasture to a hundred feet from the Mercantile's parking lot. Several of the town's buildings had been taken. Seagull Gifts, Maxine's hair salon, the Sea Horse Tavern. Seven houses and two motels. The sewage treatment plant. Most residents of Cranberry Beach now used portable toilets set up in clusters here and there around the town. The cost of the toilets would be covered by federal disaster aid. FEMA would also cover half of the rebuilding of the sewage treatment plant if the county could come up with the other half, a ridiculous notion. The county had already sunk nearly to bankruptcy years before the storm wrecked most of its infrastructure.

Mick tried not to think about what Bob Evans was going to say when he returned to his desk. But his stomach already knew it wasn't going to be good. He hoped for leniency, a generous extension of time to pay what for him amounted to an impossible sum. On his salary from the Mercantile and any Social Security benefits he would receive, it would take more than his remaining lifetime to pay it. It would take even more of Sean's lifetime if the debt were passed on to him along with the inheritance of the few remaining acres.

Mick flipped through photos from a Portland newspaper to one of Sean, on the morning after the storm, working on a rescue. Sean had driven from Portland and arrived in Cranberry Beach at first light, worried about his father. A volunteer firefighter since he was sixteen, he had grabbed his turnout clothes and reported for duty. He had been assigned to a team cutting into the top of one of the half-buried RVs. The photo showed Sean covered with mud, standing partly inside the RV, holding up a mud-matted, deranged-looking, but living poodle. Two humans had been pulled from the wreck minutes before, alive but seriously injured.

That was about an hour before Mick had arrived back in Cranberry Beach, joyously embraced by Sean before he could even step off the jet ski. Mick was proud of his son. They worked side by side for hours that morning, racing the tide to rescue people and their pets from the partially submerged RVs. Several teams of rescue workers had responded including the Coast Guard, Cranberry Beach volunteer firefighters, Sheriff's Department personnel and three search and rescue groups that had helicoptered in from Seattle. They had saved forty-two people, six dogs, a cat and a hamster. Most of the survivors had been injured in one way or another.

Sean and Mick had joined the team that crossed the channel to recover the bodies strewn among the driftwood including the two firemen in the rescue truck and Amanda and her mom. Those and the dead from the RVs had been zipped into body bags and trucked to regional hospital morgues. A man and his wife in their 80s remained unaccounted for and had been presumed washed out to sea.

Neighbors did what they could to help each other out. They got together and went house to house, nailing up blue tarps where roofs were missing and recharging freezers with gas powered generators. Teams used chainsaws to clear roads and driveways.

In the dusk of that long day the community gathered in front of the Mercantile, setting out candle lanterns and Tiki torches for light. They brought burgers and steaks from melting refrigerators to cook on charcoal and gas grills and filled tables in the street with plates of grilled vegetables, steamed clams and oysters, buns and pickles. Ice from the oyster packing plant arrived piled in the back of a pickup truck, bottles of beer packed in to cool.

The night became a sort of wake for the dead and a celebration of survival. People told stories of the storm, wept and laughed, and ate melting ice cream from the Mercantile's freezers. They put up a memorial for Tenney and Whittaker at the fire station, candles and flowers encircling their grimy, shredded turnout gear. Mick laid Amanda's butterfly hairclip among the growing array of notes and memorabilia associated with the others who had also lost their lives.

Mick yanked himself away from a line of thought that would only lead him into sentimentality and bring on tears. He looked around the office, wondering what was taking Bob so long, then despite himself slipped into memories again.

Anna had been at the wake. She had rowed over to the town in someone's aluminum rowboat. She told him how, by mid-afternoon on the day after the storm, before rescue and recovery teams had gotten across the channel, she had gone to as many houses as she could, calling out for survivors. All the humans north of Cranberry Beach except those in the dune cottages had made it out ahead of the breach. Those survivors who remained answered in meows, bleats and clucks. She had seen to their needs, reassuring them as she dragged hay from collapsed sheds, scooped feed into troughs, filled water buckets . . .

Bob's voice startled him.

"Mick, this is Jack Sullivan. Branch manager." Bob sat down in his chair and swiveled it around to look out the window.

Mick stood up and shook the hand Jack offered.

"Have a seat Mick." Jack hitched his rear onto the edge of Bob's desk and shuffled through the papers clipped into Mick's file folder.

Without raising his eyes from the papers, Jack asked, "Where are you living now?"

"In an apartment above the Mercantile." Anxiety rolled in Mick's guts.

"And you're still working there? They're still open?"

"Yes. They lost their roof but we got a new one up for them in a few days. Power was out but we still sold things. Wrote receipts by hand, made change from a cigar box."

"And what are you paying in rent for the apartment?"

"Bev isn't charging me anything at the moment."

"Okay. Good." Jack adjusted his glasses, flipped another paper. "So you can continue with your payments then."

"Well, that's what I was asking Bob about."

Bob glanced momentarily at Mick, then went back to looking out the window.

"Yes, I see." Jack closed the file folder. "You're requesting an extension on the amount of time you have to pay back our loan." He opened the folder again and looked something up. "And you want to reduce your monthly payments."

Mick felt like a beggar. "Unless there's any other alternative. My original plan to sell off some of the land to cover the loan isn't going to work now."

Jack's regretful expression didn't look genuine. "We're sorry about what happened to your property. But you've got to understand, we're as screwed as you are on that."

"Oh?" Mick was drawing a blank.

Smacking the file folder with the backs of his fingers, Jack said, "We've got no collateral to go after when you default."

A buzzy, lightheaded sensation washed over Mick. "I . . . uh . . . maybe I won't default if you lower my payments and give me longer to pay it off."

"You'll default, sooner or later. Might as well be sooner."

A hot flush of anger crept up Mick's neck and made the notch in his ear burn. "Isn't there anything else that can be done?"

Jack shrugged as he opened the file again. "Okay, you borrowed . . . what . . . $200,000? Secured by land previously appraised at $600,000, worth now—nada?"

"There are a few acres left."

"You could start by selling that."

"Who would want it? There's no way to get there. The county's not going to put in a bridge and the channel's not deep enough for a ferry."

"Well, there's our problem." Pursing his lips, Jack tossed the file folder onto Bob's desk.

For one crazy moment Mick envisioned grabbing the file folder and whacking Jack over the head with it. But he tried to think. He had taken out the loan with the expectation that he could sell a few acres of waterfront to pay it off. He never thought he would make payments on the loan for more than a few months. And he had been certain he would actually end up making money on the deal. The real estate agent had assured him that property values were heading up. The development company was getting ready to buy. But now that plan was as wrecked as the peninsula.

"What about insurance? Didn't I sign up for something like that?"

Jack shook his head and looked at Mick with an expression that didn't really come across as sympathetic. "Yeah. There's insurance. But it doesn't cover anything in the category of 'Act of God.'"

* * *

Anna frowned, listening to his story about the mortgage as she stirred the scrambled eggs in her skillet. Mick had rowed across the channel in a borrowed boat that morning with freshly ground coffee and eggs from the Mercantile and hot biscuits that Bev had baked and wrapped in a cloth napkin. Now, while Anna cooked on

72

her camp stove, he sat with Benny on the beach, enjoying the warm breeze and tropical sunshine.

He had visited her several times in the past two weeks to bring food and bottled water and to check on her safety. Which probably wasn't necessary. A few of the old-timers had returned to their homes out here on this newly created island, to houses with old-fashioned back-up facilities like outhouses and wood-burning stoves which the newer vacation homes didn't have. So there were good people around and there had been no reports of looters. Anna wasn't in any more danger living on the beach now than she was before the storm. The truth was he enjoyed her company.

She didn't buy the 'Act of God' theory of what had happened to the peninsula, which was puzzling to Mick. The storm and its effects were obvious. But Anna said she was skeptical, as a good scientist should be, but had no evidence to offer an alternative explanation.

"This sort of thing happens oftener than most people think," she said. "The ocean cuts through a barrier island in a big storm. But usually on a much smaller scale. Isabelle did it to Cape Hatteras in '03 and Irene did it again in 2011. But I don't get how it could have happened here. This peninsula is a lot more substantial than Hatteras."

"It doesn't matter *how* it happened," Mick said. "I still have to pay or they foreclose. Though I don't know what good that would do them. They wouldn't end up with anything of value."

"All that land," Anna swept her hand toward the channel, "is still yours. It's just under water right now. It'll come back some day. That's what shorelines do."

Mick smiled at her optimism. "How many years will that take—or shall I say eons? I only have two months."

"Don't worry so much. Foreclosure can take years."

"So how long before my land comes back?"

"If they dredge the navigation channel out beyond the point it might be fairly quick. They should have done that a long time ago. Part of what caused this disaster is that the channel is silted up. If they dredge it, the bay will go back to emptying out that way instead of partly here in this channel and partly up there at the point. Then the sand can start depositing over your land again and begin to mend the break."

She scooped the eggs onto three chipped ceramic dinner plates, put one down on the sand for Benny, handed one to Mick and settled down beside him. She handed him a biscuit.

"Nice dishes," Mick said. "Are you setting up housekeeping?"

"Beachcombing is good these days—or sad, really." She handed him a fork. "I think most of this stuff must have come from the dune cottages."

She pointed to a cache of canned food she had stashed in a hollow under a driftwood log. Most of the labels had been scoured away in the flood. "Chef's surprise for every dinner," she said.

Mick liked the camp she had set up in an enclosure of huge driftwood logs. She had made a roof of sticks that she could cover with a tarp if it rained. Her few dishes she scrubbed with sand and rinsed in seawater. She came into town every few days to wash her clothes at the laundromat and buy fresh fruits and vegetables from Cranberry Beach gardeners.

"Maybe I'll live on the beach too, when all my money's gone," Mick said.

She smiled and shook her head. "It's lovely to be out here in this warm weather, but it's not always nice like this. As you know."

"Maybe this is global warming. Maybe it's permanent." Mick thought that it wouldn't be such a hardship to have warmer weather. If it didn't continually spawn super-storms.

"I've been using the computer at the library to watch the sea surface temperatures. It's warm here in our channel but for months now it's been even warmer way out in the middle of the ocean, up in the Bering Sea and Gulf of Alaska. But there's no way to tell how long it's going to last, whether this is just a weather anomaly or the beginning of permanent climate change."

"Isn't climate supposed to change slowly, over thousands of years, like ice ages?"

"Under normal conditions, whatever those really are, it does. But in the past couple hundred years we humans have jiggered with a huge and complex atmospheric system that we only partly understand. We've pumped so much carbon dioxide into the air from factories and car exhaust that the natural processes that take carbon out of the air can't keep up. So carbon dioxide and other greenhouse gases keep building up and making the air warmer. The usual balancing mechanisms for heat exchange can't act fast enough to smoothly compensate for heat build-up in the atmosphere. And in the ocean."

"And that's where our storm came from?"

"Maybe. Some scientists think so, but others don't agree. Time will tell, I guess."

Mick looked west, as he and every other inhabitant of the peninsula now did several times a day, to assure himself that the sky was clear of that strangely pink, shimmering haze. Only a few of the ordinary variety of gray and white clouds floated on the horizon where the sea met the sky.

"Do you think there will be another storm like what we just had?" he asked.

"My guess would be yes, but that's only a guess, an intuition. But if one does come my bet is that this time the Weather Service will give plenty of warning."

"So we can go inland to wait it out, only to have to come back and rebuild everything again. Who has the money to do that? How can we live out here that way?"

"Plenty of people and other living beings all around the world have to cope with storms and all the other consequences of human neglect of the environment." She scowled as she gazed into the distance. "And most of them have far fewer resources than this peninsula has for dealing with the destruction. If people are going to continue living here, they're just going to have to adapt to conditions as they change, the same way all the other species of the earth have to do."

Anna's voice had gotten strident, with that righteous edge Mick associated with tree-spikers and militant environmentalists bellowing into bullhorns.

"Oops," she said. "That pained look on your face tells me I've been preaching. Sorry. I was talking about the big picture which doesn't really translate to the individual level in a situation like this. Really, I'm sorry to be talking that way."

She picked up the plates and forks and put them in a loosely woven basket, her low-tech dishwasher.

"So how's the reconstruction going?" she asked. "Are people getting back to normal yet?"

Mick relaxed. This was a much more comfortable subject of conversation. "Most of the power has been restored now on the peninsula but the sewer system is still a big problem. We probably won't get a new treatment plant any time soon so people are going to have to hook up to septic systems. Lots of homes have old septic tanks in the ground already and some folks are getting together to share systems. Most buildings have been repaired to the point of being livable again."

"Are more people getting ready to come back to their homes out here on the island?" she asked.

"It's a problem to get roofs replaced--getting building materials for that over here. The channel's too shallow to get a barge across and a bridge is out of the question for now. So people are just nailing up tarps to cover their roofs. And no one knows whether electrical power will ever be restored out here. Most of the newer houses are just about uninhabitable without electricity. And portable generators can only do so much."

"What are they going to do?"

Mick took off his glasses, rubbed his face and ran his fingers over the notch in his ear. "I don't know. Everybody's still in shock I guess. It's so hard to accept what happened, what a big change it is." He wiped his glasses on the tail of his shirt and put them back on. "Nobody can figure out what to do."

"How about you, Mick?" Anna squeezed his hand and held it. "Do you have any kind of plan yet?"

76

Mick was grateful but embarrassed. Her kindness nudged him close to tears.

"I guess I've got to find out about bankruptcy or something. There's no way I can pay what I owe. And I can't support Sean anymore either, that's the worst part."

"Maybe that's not such a bad thing for Sean. A young man needs to be responsible for himself. It's part of growing up."

"Yeah. I can see that." Mick's voice broke and tears threatened but he kept talking. "He told me yesterday that he's transferring to community college next month and he's going to pay for it himself. For now he's staying at Stew Johnston's, working from morning 'till night helping people on the peninsula rebuild. There's a lot of work and he's saving money."

"I don't think you have to worry about that boy," Anna said, smiling. She patted his hand and let it go.

"You're probably right. But I was so scared for him when he was arrested. Julie and I were both blindsided. And I've been worried ever since, wanting to help him, wanting to steer him away from the bad road he was on. I had always thought he would inherit the house and land so he would have something of his own. But . . ." Mick fought back a sob. So unmanly to cry.

"Have you told him what you told me during the storm?"

"No. Not yet. The time hasn't been right." Mick had thought about it, but couldn't bear the possibility that Sean might turn away from him in disgust. Not just now anyway. Maybe later when things settle down.

He glanced away, blinking tears. A change of subject was necessary.

"You know, I never heard what happened with your blue houseboat," he said.

Anna got up and brushed sand off her shorts. "I only saw it for about five minutes," she said. "It swept right past on the current, out of the bay and into the ocean."

"Any turtles show up?"

The subject of the Turtle Lady, when it came up in the Mercantile, was usually accompanied by rolling eyes and scoffing.

Mick continued to defend her, though he was as skeptical as anyone else.

"No turtles. Not yet."

Anna shaded her eyes with her hand, watching a boat crossing the channel.

"Have you heard about Marvin Younger?" she asked.

"From that real estate development company? Yeah. I heard he's been talking to people with land out here."

"Has he talked to you yet?"

"No. But I haven't got much land. No one would want it."

Anna smiled and raised an eyebrow. "Your land may actually be worth a lot more than you think."

She got her binoculars out of her pack and watched as two men beached the aluminum Boston Whaler several hundred yards away.

"The bulldozer man," she said.

Mick heard an edge of anger in her voice. He took the binoculars when she passed them to him.

"Boris," he said. "And Jim Oakley. That's his fishing boat. I wonder what they're up to."

"Have you seen the bulldozer?" Anna pointed to a spot in the middle of the channel. "You can row over there and look down into the water and see it at low tide."

She took the binoculars back and watched the men walk up the beach to the broken edge of the road.

"I don't like that guy," she said.

"Which one?"

"The one who was rearranging the beach with the bulldozer."

"Nobody likes him."

After a few minutes of watching the men, Anna said, "Looks like they're doing something at the corner of your fence."

By the time Mick and Anna had made their way over the driftwood and climbed up onto the road, the two men had driven a wooden stake into the sod of the county road right-of-way at the north end of Mick's fence. Boris squatted as he held the end tab of a tape measure on the stake while Oakley walked south, playing out the hundred-foot tape. When it was fully extended he marked the spot with another stake.

Oakley greeted Mick affably as he turned the handle to roll the tape back into the case. Mick introduced Anna.

"So you're the Turtle Lady." Oakley, grinning under his neatly trimmed blonde mustache, shifted his hammer to his left hand and extended his right hand to shake Anna's. "Heard a lot about you, how you two survived the storm surge out there on the point."

Oakley's glance at Mick had a bit of a leer in it.

"Find any turtles yet?" he said to Anna.

Mick didn't like the snicker that was part of Oakley's supposedly friendly smile. Anna just shook her head and shrugged. It was Benny who expressed his low opinion by growling, not at Oakley but at Boris who walked toward them.

Anna quieted Benny with a word.

"Is that the corner of your property?" Oakley asked, pointing to the first stake he had set where the barbed wire fence paralleling the road made a right-angle turn.

"More or less. What are you doing?"

"Just getting a rough indication of the property lines—for an interested party. The official surveyors will be here next week."

"But my land's not even for sale. Who's doing the survey?"

Oakley bent to pound the stake in further with the hammer. "Not at liberty to say at this point."

"Marvin Younger," Mick guessed. "Are you working for him?"

Oakley straightened up, breathing hard from his work. "Not exactly."

The exact nature of Jim Oakley's employment was unclear to most residents of Cranberry Beach. He had business that caused him to travel out of town a lot, invariably taking his golf clubs with him. And he seemed to be owner/developer of the cluster of vacation homes formerly called the dune cottages, now wrecked and strewn for miles along the beach.

And as chief, he was the only paid member of the Cranberry Beach Volunteer Fire Department, though he often didn't respond to emergency calls and regularly assigned his assistant chief to do the paperwork and run the weekly drills.

He had, however, risen to the role of TV spokesman in the frantic hours after the storm, his square jaw and blonde mustache dramatically mud-splattered as he reported from a makeshift podium. But his directions to the rescue crews had been generally ignored. The commander of one of the out-of-town search and rescue units actually took charge of coordinating operations.

Oakley had qualified for the fire chief job because his resume stated prior experience in a small town fire department. Mick knew someone in the county human resources department who knew that Oakley's references hadn't been thoroughly checked. He was friendly and outgoing and talked like he knew what he was doing. But it was only because of Mick's willingness to pick up the slack that Oakley got away with his half-assed job performance.

Not that the part-time fire chief's pay was anything to write home about. The extra few hundred bucks per month would have made a difference in Mick's monthly budget—before the storm. But it was nothing in the context of Oakley's lifestyle. A drop in the bucket of what Oakley's fancy four-bedroom house on the ridge must have cost.

Mick looked to the west, trying to visualize the vicinity's pre-storm geography.

"Are you marking off the property line for the dune cottages too?" he asked.

"Yeah. I'll go off your property line. But I'm afraid there's nothing left. Maybe a few feet along the channel beach. But the road that went out to the dunes is completely gone."

"So you lost everything too," Mick said.

"Yep. The dune cottages anyway. My house is okay."

"But your investment. You've got to owe big money like I do."

Oakley looked blank for a minute. "Oh. Yeah. Big money."

"What are you going to do? File for bankruptcy?"

Boris arrived, inspiring another growl from Benny. He reached for the tab end of the measuring tape, squatted and held it against the wooden stake.

Oakley picked up the hammer, tucked the remaining stakes under his arm, and started backing slowly away from the Russian, letting the tape unwind from the case.

"Bankruptcy? No, I've got other—options."

Mick and Anna walked along the road with Oakley.

"If I were you, Mick, I would accept what Marvin Younger offers," Oakley said. "It might be your best solution."

"Or it might not," Anna interjected.

Oakley stopped moving to regard Mick and Anna with wide eyes and slack jaw.

"What Marvin Younger has to offer us is going to be the best thing that ever happened to this peninsula," he said.

"Let me guess," Anna said, icing up with sarcasm. "A resort. A big resort."

Oakley grinned. "I can neither confirm nor deny."

"So the dune cottages are nothing compared to what's going to come in if Younger can buy up the land out here."

"Again, I can't say anything right now . . . but someday people are going to say this storm wasn't such a disaster."

Anna's eyes turned a cold steel blue. "Amanda wouldn't say that. Or her mom. Or the other people who died because they were not safe in houses *you* built too close to the surf."

Oakley resumed backing up, letting the tape play out. A pink flush colored his throat and his lips were drawn into a tight line.

"I don't know what you're talking about."

Anna was on a roll. "Shoreline development laws. Structures can't be built that close to the beach, for obvious reasons. I don't know how you got away with it."

Trouble flickered across Oakley's face but he rearranged it to a semblance of indignant innocence.

"Got away with what? All my permits were signed off by the county. No other government agencies made any effort to even look at my project." The measuring tape stopped, fully extended again.

Oakley scuffed the gravel with his heel to mark the place and reached for another wooden stake.

"People want to be able to see the ocean from the windows of their vacation cottage," he said. "And they're happy to pay extra for that privilege. This storm—the way it wrecked everything," he waved the stake toward the new channel, "was a freak of nature. Beyond anyone's control. The dune cottages would have been fine in any kind of normal storm."

Benny growled again and Anna frowned as she watched Boris stride toward them.

"No, that's not true. The bulldozing," she said, pointing at Boris. "The way he pushed sand up around the cottages probably magnified the effect of the waves. A long, flat beach backed by a series of natural dunes dissipates wave energy during a severe storm. But what he did, the way he scraped sand off the lower beach and moved it to the area around the mouth of the creek, would have made even ordinary storm waves more dangerous. They would have broken nearer to the cottages and with much more power on the steepened beach. I assume he did it under your orders."

Boris arrived, scowling, and grumbled something in Russian. He took the hammer from Oakley and drove the stake into the ground with three efficient blows.

"I was only replacing sand that had disappeared from around the cottages because of what the Army Corps of Engineers is doing down at the river mouth," Oakley said. "That is my right and there's no law against it. If I hadn't done it the cottages would have been undercut in a couple years. I was just protecting my investment."

"Moving the sand that way is probably what destroyed your investment—and several lives." Anna's voice was steady and serious and her blue eyes shone like beacons.

Oakley smiled and shook his head. He winked at Mick, as if sharing the knowledge that this lady was just another flaky environmentalist.

"Ma'am," he said, holding up both hands in a gesture of giving up, "I think we've just got to agree to disagree on that."

82

Impatient, Boris took the tape from Oakley and fastened the end tab to the stake with a small nail he dug out of his pocket. But something in the way he paused for a second and studied Anna's face suggested to Mick that Boris was listening carefully. Maybe he understood more English than he let on. He walked backwards, letting the tape roll out until he reached the broken edge of the road where he lay the tape case down.

While Oakley went to record the measurement in his notebook, Boris strode onto the beach, squatted to dig a bit of debris out of the sand, examined it briefly and tossed it aside.

"Another beachcomber," Mick said to Anna as they walked back toward her camp. He had seen Boris several times after the storm, walking the beach on both sides of the channel, poking around in the piles of flotsam, occasionally digging something small out of the sand. But unlike other beachcombers out for salvage or curios, Boris was never seen carrying anything.

Out of his sight behind a driftwood stump, Anna watched Boris with her binoculars. "He's looking for something," she said. "Something in particular."

6

Mary Eggers pulled up the hood of her pink sweatshirt to protect her freshly permed hair from a light, wind-driven rain. She walked west along the shoulder of Fairhaven road farther than her daily outing customarily took her. Usually she turned back toward her home at Seagull Circle before getting into this neighborhood of rundown shacks and shabby trailer houses. But Lucky had run ahead with a purpose, jumped the drainage ditch that edged the road and disappeared into the brush of scrub pine and alder saplings.

"Lucky, come on now!" Mary called her dog for the fourth time, fingering the leash in her pocket. She usually allowed him to run free on their walks but had the leash in case they met up with other dogs. He had a tendency to pick fights.

Peering into the dense brush, she strained to see a glimpse of his brown-speckled fur. A driveway of rutted, sandy mud cut through the pines in the general direction Lucky had gone. She couldn't see beyond the first curve of the drive. Hesitating, she looked around at the dingy shacks along the road. Wrecked cars and rusting kitchen appliances slouched in yards scattered with storm debris. A short-haired, big-headed brindle dog yanked on his chain and lifted his nose to get a smell of her.

Mary thought of turning around and walking home without Lucky, but the last time he had been out by himself he had crawled home with the skin dangling from a serious gash on his neck. The vet said if it had been a half-inch deeper he would have been dead.

Pulling the corners of her sweatshirt together, she zipped it up, wishing she had stayed home knitting this morning instead of taking the damned dog out. She checked to be sure her phone was in her pocket before stepping off the road onto the muddy driveway. Afraid of surprising anyone who might object to her trespassing, she called loudly to Lucky as she walked.

The storm had deposited odds and ends of things in the thicket of pine and alder that pushed up to both sides of the driveway—a muddy kitchen curtain, some grayish men's underwear, shreds of black tar paper, twisted plastic rain gutters. Someone's sneaker lay flattened in the mud, run over by cars. Mary knew that these things would never be collected by the owners or tenants of these lots and carted off to the dump the way Mary and her neighbors had done. In this neighborhood the leavings of the storm would become just another part of the depressing landscape. Publicly, Mary would say the people who lived here were afflicted with low self-esteem. Privately she called them lowlifes.

84

She looked over her shoulder. Fairhaven Road was now out of sight beyond the curve in the driveway. When she looked forward again there was Lucky, coming toward her in a half-slink, his ears down and head turned to glance behind him.

Taking the leash out of her pocket, she called to him. The sight and jingle of it usually caused him to rush enthusiastically to have it snapped onto his collar. But this time he sunk onto his belly until Mary got close enough to lean down and reach for his collar. He eluded her grasp, turned and crept farther down the driveway, eyes sharp, ears forward, the hair on the top of his neck bristling. He glanced to see if Mary would follow.

"Lucky, get over here," she whispered. She took a few steps to see where he had gone. The dog's demeanor made her own neck tingle. This was a neighborhood where violence was common.

When she rounded the curve she saw Lucky a little distance beyond her. He stood stiff-legged, head down, nose stretched to sniff at what looked like a pile of clothes in the middle of the drive. A growl rumbled in his chest.

"For heaven's sake, Lucky, what *is* that?"

Without moving closer she stared at it for a minute until she finally got the sense of what she saw there. With trembling hands, she took the phone out of her pocket and pressed 9-1-1.

* * *

Mick Mahoney sat in the cab of the new rescue truck fumbling for the windshield wiper controls. The truck had been loaned to Cranberry Beach by one of the Olympia area volunteer departments and this was the first day of rain since the big storm. He hadn't needed to use the windshield wipers until now. But he couldn't find a lever in the intuitive place on the steering column.

"Shit." He adjusted his glasses to peer at the switches and buttons on the dash.

No other volunteers had arrived yet at the fire station in response to the "man down" call. The department was short-handed now without Tenney and Whittaker. Most of the other volunteers worked at jobs off the peninsula and weren't available for daytime calls. Aware of seconds passing, he flipped various levers and switches, activating everything from turn signals to emergency lights, but not the wipers.

Few details had accompanied the dispatcher's call. It could be anything from a simple fall, or an elderly person without the strength to get up, to a life-and-death situation—cardiac arrest, stroke, drug overdose. A few minutes could make all the difference in someone's survival. Mick couldn't wait any longer for another EMT firefighter to ride with him in the rescue truck. He had to go even if he couldn't see very well through the windshield.

He hit the siren, put the truck in gear, and rolled onto the main road with both windows down to check for traffic. The rain wasn't heavy but it shimmied across the windshield on a stiff wind off the ocean. Between gear shiftings he steered with his left hand and slapped around the steering column with his right. Something connected. The wipers came on.

Now that he could see, he thought about where he was going.

The dispatcher had said a woman would be on Fairhaven road to show him the driveway. He remembered the place from a domestic violence call a few months ago. A woman had been kicked in the ribs and had trouble breathing. Collapsed lung. Her name was Meredith-something. Frizzy blonde hair. Her roomie had aimed his boot at the snake tattooed on her chest. They had treated her out in the yard so Mick hadn't seen the inside of the junky house trailer at the end of the driveway.

After a two-minute run down the main highway, he downshifted and made the right turn onto Fairhaven, a graveled side road that dead-ended in a cluster of what had once been clam diggers' shacks, now serving as the peninsula's slum district.

Mick recognized Mary Eggers waiting at the side of the road with her dog on a leash. She motioned to where he should turn onto the unmarked driveway. He waved at her and steered toward the strobe lights flashing through the trees from the Sheriff's department car.

He bounced the rescue truck along the mucky ruts of the driveway, hoping he remembered correctly that there was a turn-around down by the trailer. It would be hard to back all the way out.

Which was probably what he would have to do. For some reason, the deputy's green and white county SUV was angled across the driveway about a hundred feet before its end, preventing Mick from going farther. He parked, grabbed the jump kit from a compartment in the side of the truck, and side-stepped between the police car and the thick brush.

Sheriff's Deputy Rick Harmon, talking to dispatch on his shoulder-mounted radio, waved Mick over with a free arm and pointed to the ground near his feet. A human sprawled motionless, face down. Male, young, dressed in jeans and sneakers. The back of the T-shirt had a dark hole in the middle of it.

Harmon put a hand up to slow Mick's sprint and called out, "Take your time, Mick, he's dead."

The deputy's radio crackled a burst of static. Harmon listened and answered the dispatcher tersely, turning to look at the trailer house as he spoke.

"Nobody home but the door was wide open. It's a meth lab," he said to Mick. "I think we're far enough away to deal with this guy, but don't go any closer to the house. I've called Hazmat. They should be here in twenty minutes. And I notified the medical examiner."

"Ah, Geez. I hate this," Mick said as he kneeled beside the body, pulling on his latex gloves. He had to determine for himself whether he could agree with Harmon that the subject was deceased. It was possible a tiny flame of life still flickered somewhere inside and if so, it was Mick's responsibility to do everything he could to keep it burning.

He brushed aside the longish dark brown hair and pressed two fingers to the side of the neck. His own heart skipped and he felt a tightening in his chest. There was something achingly familiar about this young man, the angular forearm, the long fingers. Hair just like this.

There was not even the faintest ticking in the carotid artery. The skin was cold and gray and wet from the rain. The tooled leather belt, a pattern of interwoven Celtic knots, was so like the one Sean wore. Mick's hands shook as he lifted the hair from the face, found the berry-shaped brown birthmark on the cheek.

"Oh, God. Oh, Jesus," he moaned. "Help me turn him over."

The front of the T-shirt was blackly clotted with blood and dirt. No bright red, oxygenated blood rushed out. Only a seep of damp, smelly goo.

"Oh, damn, Mick," Harmon said. "Is it Sean?"

Mick studied the face, not quite seeing Sean in it, transformed as it was by death. But the thick, dark hair, the chip out of the upper tooth, the favorite belt, the hammer-blackened left thumb he had displayed for his father two days ago, all confirmed identification.

Harmon kneeled and pulled a wallet out of the back pocket of the jeans.

"Mick," he said. "Here's his driver's license. It's Sean. Oh, shit, Mick. I'm so sorry."

"What the hell happened?" Mick could barely get the words out.

Harmon stood up, took out a phone and keyed in a number. "This kind of shit happens all the time at drug houses," he said.

Mick heard him say Sheriff Grayson's name into the phone before the deputy turned away to speak privately.

Thirty-five intolerable minutes of silence and rain passed before Mick heard the parade of sirens out on the main road. Hazmat and the Sheriff came from Spencer's Landing, the county seat on the other side of the bay. And the medical examiner drove up from the county hospital, fifteen miles south. All the responders had gotten the word already about Sean.

Dr. Alex Landers, the ME, took a minute to squat beside Mick before getting to work.

"Your kid, huh?"

"Yeah." Mick sat cross-legged holding Sean's body in his lap. His eyes had kept returning to the ragged exit wound in Sean's chest, gradually allowing the reality of death to sink in, in a tearless and objective way. But he couldn't accept that Sean had gotten back into drugs.

"It's tough to lose a child," Landers said, encircling Mick's shoulders with his arm. "I know how it is. It's the worst."

Tears flooded Mick's face now.

"Okay. You know I've got to do my job now. I need your help."

Landers squeezed Mick's shoulder and stood up.

"We need to get the body back in the position where it was found. Can you help me do that?"

Mick was grateful for the task, something he could understand. He and Landers and Harmon carefully repositioned the body as the Hazmat team trooped past in their moon suits.

Landers wrote something in his notebook. "Is this where he was when Mrs. Eggers saw him?"

Harmon nodded.

"Hmm. Interesting. Not enough blood on the ground under him. He was killed somewhere else." Landers got a camera out of his bag.

"There's nothing more you can do for him now," he said to Mick. "My office will let you know when he's ready for funeral arrangements. It's hard to do, I know, but you're going to have to leave now."

"I know he wasn't doing drugs."

"We're going to have to do tests for that," Landers said.

"One thing," Mick said. "Just . . . can you tell me . . ." Tears pulled him up short.

"Did he suffer?" Landers provided the words Mick couldn't say. "Not for long. It's a big wound, big caliber weapon. Matter of seconds I would think, if not immediate unconsciousness."

* * *

That evening Mick hung up the phone and leaned back into the couch cushions, exhausted and heartsick. It was the second time he had talked with Julie since the wrenching call he had made to her

89

from the scene that morning. She had refused to let him come to Astoria. But she had called him at his apartment two times so far, trying to piece together in her own mind the staggering fact of Sean's death.

Nothing Mick could say would sway her belief that Sean had gotten back into using drugs, or selling them. She blamed his friends, lack of discipline in his high school, and the criminal element he undoubtedly had encountered in prison. And irrationally, she also blamed the legalization of marijuana. She batted away Mick's attempts to defend Sean in favor of a harsh but clear and simple explanation she could accept and begin to live with. Though it was unfair to Sean, Mick could see her need for clarity. He was nearly unhinged himself.

And now he could hear by the creaking of the stairs that someone was coming up from the Mercantile to his apartment. Probably Bev again, bringing a cake or pie to go with the homemade beef stew she had put into his refrigerator that afternoon. Food, for Bev, meant love.

It was the love that had done him in. He had wanted to work, to escape through ordinary routine the anguish of the morning's events. But because so many people came into the store that afternoon to express their sympathy, Bev had made him sit down in one of the folding chairs by the coffee maker. Every time someone pressed his hand or hugged him and said "I'm sorry," Mick had teared up. It wasn't something he could control.

When he opened the door and saw it was Anna who stood there with a bag of groceries, her face wet with tears, the last remaining thread of his self-control broke and he gave in to sobbing, wailing grief.

Later, Anna made hot, sweet tea. He was grateful for her quiet company.

"There's nothing left for me here," Mick said, his head stuffy and dull. "Nothing to keep me here now. I'll sell what's left of the land and go—I don't know where. Montana maybe."

Mick put his cup down and rubbed his puffy face then picked up his glasses from the side table and put them back on. Anna sat in the easy chair across from him with Benny snoozing on her lap. She held a mug of tea in both hands, her eyes closed. She had captured her hair in a blue bandana, wore jeans and a light blue work shirt, the sleeves rolled up to the elbows. She hadn't said anything at all since she arrived, had sat with him quietly the whole time he had been sobbing.

"Anna?"

She opened her eyes, red like his own must be.

"I'm going to sell it. The land. Get whatever I can then get out of here. No forwarding address."

"What's in Montana?"

Mick had picked Montana out of the air. "Mountains I guess. I haven't seen many mountains."

"People in Montana dream about seeing the ocean," she said.

Anna got up, went to the kitchen and took Bev's foil-wrapped casserole out of the refrigerator. Mick watched as she slid it into the oven, set the heat control, and rummaged in the kitchen drawers.

"Do you have a corkscrew?" she asked.

They sipped wine as the fragrance of Bev's stew wafted out from the kitchen. It was comforting to talk of mundane things.

"The insurance on the Suburban isn't going to pay for towing it out from under all those trees. And even if we got it free of the trees, there's no way to get it over to this side. The agent says it's probably a total loss but they won't cut a check until he can get over to see it."

Mick felt his spirits flagging again, and his voice broke. "Which might be never as far as they care."

"You've had a lot of losses in a short amount of time, Mick."

The reminder cut a fresh hole into his grief.

"Things will look different in a few weeks," she said when he had mopped his eyes again and blown his nose. "When my husband died—Daniel—it was so sudden. I wasn't really thinking right. But you come around. You're never quite mended, but you get on with life."

Mick couldn't see how.

"Sean was a good kid," he said. "It's just . . . I just don't get it. It's such a bad thing that happened to him. The Sheriff says they all get back into drugs once they start. He said Sean must have gone back to selling, got involved with the meth trade or something. Said getting shot is one of the hazards of the business."

Anna shook her head slowly.

"But I don't know, I just don't think he was doing that," Mick said. "Hell, he's been too busy working."

"Hold onto that intuition," Anna said. "You may be the only person who can find out what really happened."

7

He and Anna had stayed up late talking. After she and Benny curled up with a blanket on the couch, Mick had lain motionless and wakeful in his bed for hours. Sleep didn't come until the sky lightened toward dawn. When he woke, late for work, fog had rolled in and Anna and Benny were gone. He made coffee and stared into the blank, white fog. Nothing left. No son, no wife—no living relatives for that matter. No home, no land. No money. Big debt.

Anna had listed the things he did have: a job, friends, a respected place in the community. And she had insisted that his land wasn't gone. Not completely.

They had talked about the real estate development company and what its agent, Marvin Younger, might be prepared to offer Mick. Anna had made him promise he wouldn't make any immediate decisions.

Last night, woolly-headed with wine and grief, he had agreed that it would be reasonable to wait a couple weeks before doing anything. But this morning, tired and bereft, Mick thought that maybe Marvin Younger would offer enough to pay off the loan. That was all he hoped for.

It wasn't long before Younger's business card was in Mick's shirt pocket. Younger came into the Mercantile in the early afternoon, introduced himself with a cordial handshake and murmured a brief, conventional expression of sympathy for Mick's loss. Then he asked if there was somewhere they could talk.

Upstairs in the apartment, Mick sat across the kitchen table from a young man with a stylish haircut, wearing a suit and tie and carrying a briefcase. Younger announced that SeaMist, the corporation he represented, was interested in buying some of the property on the new island with the intention of holding it for possible future development. A long-term investment. They wondered whether Mick was interested in selling, to offset some of the mortgage they knew he carried.

"Not the whole mortgage?" Mick asked, a pang of disappointment twitching in his stomach.

Younger got a pad of yellow, lined paper out of his briefcase. Handwritten notes and numbers crammed the pages. He circled something, looked up at Mick, pursed his lips regretfully, and tapped the numbers with his pen. "You probably know better than I do how much of your land is left after the breach. I've made some preliminary calculations. The survey will be done in a few days, then we'll know more. But what I come up with now, roughly, is that you have about five acres of dry land left."

Mick couldn't argue with that.

"Five acres, at five thousand an acre, would give you $25,000."

"That doesn't help me much," Mick said.

"Better than nothing." Younger flipped pages. "But maybe we could up it a little if we include what's under water."

"Why would anyone want that?"

"No one would. You'd have a helluva time selling it to anyone else. But SeaMist has a slight interest in it, for future use."

"Oh," Mick said. A lightbulb of comprehension went on in his head. "A bridge. Before you build a resort or whatever you have planned you've got to have a bridge."

"Or a causeway. But we don't have to build it yet. No hurry. If we decide to go ahead with development we can get the county to build a bridge. Tax revenues would more than justify it. They would simply use the existing county road right-of-way. But if you want to sell the underwater portion of your land to us now, we might be amenable to that, if the price is reasonable."

"What's your offer?"

94

Younger consulted his notes again. "What's your mortgage? $200,000? We could work with that number. For the whole parcel, dry and wet."

He took a document from his briefcase. Mick could see that his name had already been typed on a line labeled "seller."

Later in the day Mick took a break, sitting with Anna and Benny in the shade of the Mercantile's porch. The real estate document raised Anna's hackles. It wasn't signed. Though tempted to accept SeaMist's offer on the spot and be done with it, Mick wanted to stay in Anna's good graces. He had told Younger he wanted to take some time to think about it, which had clearly pissed Younger off. Mick wondered why, since Younger had said SeaMist wasn't in a hurry.

"There's something odd here," Anna said, tapping the figure Younger had penned in. "I've been talking to the other property owners on the island. Nobody has gotten such a generous offer as this. Everybody I've talked to says the offers are rock-bottom. Insulting. But there aren't many other options for the people out there. SeaMist has a considerable advantage.

"Maybe they think if I sell the others will too."

"That's probably exactly what they're hoping."

"But why do they want *all* my land—including what's underwater?"

"I keep trying to tell you." Anna sounded like she was trying to be patient with him. "Gradually the break will fill in and someday there's going to be a gorgeous beach there. Especially if SeaMist builds a dike-like structure that will speed up deposition of sand. They'd much rather pay you what seems like a huge amount now than have to pay what it's really going to be worth sometime in the near future."

Mick pushed his glasses up on his forehead and rubbed his face with his hands. "Can you be more specific on that timeline? I just don't know how I can afford to hold out. In a few more weeks I won't be able to make the mortgage payments anymore."

"SeaMist knows that."

"Shit."

Anna folded the document and returned it to Mick, then shaded her eyes to look at the western sky. The fog had burnt off before ten that morning and although the calendar said it was late September, the temperature was nearing ninety at four o'clock. It wouldn't be heading back down for another hour or so. A stiff wind should have been cooling but it felt gritty and brought no relief from the heat.

"The sky looks funny again," Mick said.

"That yellowish haze? That's dust from last week's dust storm in central China. They've had a tough summer. Drought."

"And I suppose that's from global warming too?"

She shot him an exasperated glance.

"I wonder what SeaMist is offering Oakley," Mick said, to change the subject.

"Oh!" Anna looked like she remembered something important. She dug around in her backpack and took out a spiral notebook.

"I was at the library this morning working with Loretta on the internet. We were using the county tax assessor's website to get names of landowners on the new island."

"Why?"

"Because I want to find them and talk to them about not giving in to SeaMist."

"That's asking a lot." He didn't understand why she would want to do this but he was beginning to admire her persistence.

"I know," Anna said. There was something very determined in her gaze. "But I've got to try. This development could turn into a very bad thing for the community. And I know a lot of people here— most of them—probably think I'm really only concerned about turtle habitat, which sounds crazy to them. But when I talk about *community* I mean *all living beings,* not just humans."

Mick wondered what the definition of crazy was and whether Anna qualified. And whether he was crazy himself for liking her.

"Anyway—guess what?"

"What?"

96

"This is what we found out. The dune cottages? SeaMist already owned them before the storm."

It took a few minutes for that to sink in. Oakley had always acted like owner/developer. But all along he must have been working for SeaMist.

"Not only that—SeaMist owns Oakley's house too."

Benny came to attention with ears forward as the piercing cries of a child interrupted their conversation. A deeply tanned man wearing shorts and no shirt hurried up the path from the beach toward the Mercantile, carrying a toddler wrapped in a beach towel. The child flailed his arms and legs, and his face was red from screaming. The man's look of panic told Mick this was some kind of medical emergency.

Anna and Bev and a couple of customers clustered around them as Mick and the man laid the little boy down in the shade on the floor of the porch.

"My son was playing on the beach with his cousins," the father shouted over his son's screaming. "The bigger kids were wading with him in the edge of the surf, dipping him in and out of the small waves. Then Harry started screaming. Nobody can get any words out of him."

Mick went through the EMT's checklist. Breathing: yes— vigorous. Bleeding: no. Pulse: fast and strong. Eyes: flooded with tears but pupils equal and reactive. Broken bones or bruises: no. There was no difference in the child's response when Mick gently pressed his limbs and abdomen. He removed the towel from around the child's body and turned him over. A red, curving line whipped along the skin of the back of the leg from hip to ankle.

"Jellyfish sting," Anna said. "The tentacle is still there. I can get it."

Her hand covered with an edge of the towel she carefully grasped a nearly invisible blue thread that adhered to the boy's skin along the course of the red welt. When she pulled it away Mick could see it was about three feet long. She rolled it up in the corner of the towel.

"We've got to check him for more," she said. "And we'll need water to rinse him off. And some ice."

"What about vinegar? That's good for jellyfish stings," Bev called as she lurched inside, hurrying as best she could on her arthritic knees.

"No vinegar—not for this kind of sting," Anna called back.

Bev returned with two one-gallon containers of drinking water. Mick broke the seals, pried off the lids and sloshed the water over the boy's skin. Anna inspected him for more tentacles. She found one stuck to his shorts, pulled it off with another edge of the towel and wrapped it up.

"We've got to get his shorts off," Anna called after Bev who had hustled back into the store for ice. "Do you have another towel we could use?"

Bev appeared again in a few minutes with crushed ice in three zipped plastic bags and a new beach towel from the Mercantile's shelves. A few minutes later Harry relaxed in his father's arms, iced and wrapped in the big, colorful beach towel, sobbing intermittently.

Anna frowned as she examined the long blue tentacles. "I need to get a look at this jellyfish."

When they were sure Harry showed no signs of severe allergic reaction to the sting, Mick and Anna left him to recover with the help of an ice cream bar. Anna gathered several spray bottles from the Mercantile and filled them with water. Then she confirmed with Mick that the rescue truck carried epinephrine injectors.

A few minutes later, as Mick drove the rescue truck onto the beach, he glanced at Anna in the passenger seat. "What kind of jellyfish do you think that was?"

"Nothing native to the north Pacific has such a long blue tentacle. In fact, there's only one I know of that does and it lives in tropical waters. And if that's what stung little Harry, we've got a serious problem."

Mick parked the truck on the hard-packed sand and followed Anna as she paced the beach at the edge of the small, foamy wavelets of spent surf. She had put on Mick's turnout boots to protect her feet and legs and she wore latex gloves, a long-sleeved shirt and long jeans. She carried a plastic 5-gallon bucket. Mick, dressed in shorts and sandals, and barefooted Benny, were admonished to stay out of the water.

No one else was in the water as far as Mick could see up and down the beach. Maybe word had gotten around about the jellyfish sting. But several groups of people clustered here and there on the upper beach, and he would have to warn them soon about the potential danger. It would be easier if Anna could find something definitive.

She bent and dug in the wet sand, tugging at a length of plastic covered wire. Holding it up for Mick to see, she asked, "What is this anyway? I've seen pieces of this here and there all over the beach after the storm."

Mick took a look. "That's blasting wire. What you use to set off dynamite. Blowing stumps, things like that."

"Why would it be on the beach?"

"Just litter from the storm I guess. It's a common enough thing in rural areas. There was probably a roll of it forgotten in some farmer's barn."

Anna coiled it and stuffed it in the back pocket of her jeans, gazing at the channel the ocean had cut through the peninsula.

"Holy shit!" She jumped back from something that washed over her feet in a surging wavelet.

It was translucent, with a gooey-looking gob of gelatinous blue stuff attached.

Anna positioned the bucket seaward of the creature and allowed the next wave backwash to push it in. With her gloved hands she coaxed in the long train of coiled blue tentacles.

It righted itself so that the body section floated on the surface of the water in the bucket, its mess of blue stuff hanging down below it. The body part had a vertical, six-inch crest running along its top.

"That's a gas-filled float that acts like a kind of sail," Anna said. "The wind pushes it from place to place."

"I've never seen anything like that around here. What is it?"

"A bluebottle. That's one name for it. They can be dangerous. Some people are very sensitive to the sting."

She peeled her gloves off, dropped them into the bucket with the jellyfish, and picked up the binoculars that hung around her neck. She studied the area of water beyond the surf line.

"Why is it here now?" Mick asked, squatting beside the bucket with Benny to cautiously examine the beast.

She swung the binoculars to study a different part of the surf.

"This creature is normally found in tropical waters. They're well known in the Hawaiian Islands where they're blown onto the beaches in huge swarms when the wind is right. Like it is here today."

Mick squinted against the lowering sun, looking for floating, bottle-like creatures.

"Are there any more out there?"

Anna put the binoculars down. "Yeah. Probably hundreds."

"Okay," Mick said as he turned and headed for the rescue truck. "I'll call the Sheriff's department. They'll probably want to close the beach."

Anna carried the bucket up the beach to where the truck was parked and as Mick leaned into the cab talking to the dispatcher on the radio, she photographed the creature with her phone. Then she put on a new pair of latex gloves and lifted the bluebottle out of the bucket. Setting it on a thick pad of paper towels on the edge of the truck's tailgate, she arranged it so the tentacles trailed down into the bucket. She photographed it again that way, lowered it back into the bucket, stripped her gloves off, and keyed a number into her phone.

"Maury," she said, "It's Anna. I've got a specimen of Physalia in a bucket here at Cranberry Beach. You know, a bluebottle. Like we saw in Maui." She listened, looking uneasily at the sea for a few minutes, then spoke again.

"I can see plenty more beyond the surf line. I'm sending you photos . . . yes, I think they're going to close the beaches . . ." She looked to Mick for confirmation and he nodded. "Call me when you know more. Thanks."

Anna closed the cover on the phone and put it away.

"My coworker at the National Marine Fisheries. He's going to pass the info on to the appropriate department. They'll probably have people down here tomorrow morning. Quite an interesting development."

"Your coworker," Mick said, confused. "You have a job?"

He backpedaled when Anna raised an eyebrow. "I mean, I thought you were just . . . a retired . . . uh . . ."

"Just a wacky turtle lady?"

Mick had been getting the impression lately that she was much more than that.

"No—I guess I don't really know what you do."

"I don't mind being thought of as a nut, people leave me alone. But I really do have a job. I'm a NOAA biologist. I work at that for about nine months of the year. During the summers I take leave without pay and do my own research."

The dispatcher's voice erupted from the radio. Mick answered briefly and replaced the handset in its cradle.

"I've got to try to keep people out of the water until the Sheriff's department gets here." Mick shaded his eyes to look down the beach. "Some people are headed for the surf now. Gotta go."

Anna shouted first aid instructions for jellyfish sting over the brassy din of the engine. "Pick off the tentacles with gloves. No vinegar, alcohol, urine, meat tenderizer. Nothing like that. Rinse with clear water from the spray bottles, don't just dunk people in the surf to wash them off, there might be more tentacles in the seawater. They should get checked out by a doctor if they get a rash or signs of infection. Cortisone or Benadryl can ease the pain and swelling. And watch for anaphylactic shock. Some people are so sensitive to the venom that they just conk out and stop breathing. They've got to get the epinephrine right away."

"Okay, hopefully we won't have to do that," Mick shouted as he switched on the flashing lights and put the truck in gear.

"And tell them not to step on or touch the dead ones that wash up on the beach. The toxins can remain potent for several hours."

"Right. Bluebottles. Is that what you said they're called?"

"Yes," Anna called out as he pulled away. "Another name for them is Portuguese Man-of-War."

Mick put on the brakes and leaned out the window. "Now *that* I've heard of."

"That's what we've got."

"Holy shit."

8

Two days later, as another hot afternoon cooled to dusk, Mick jammed on the brakes and cut the siren and lights. Skidding on loose gravel, he swung the rescue truck into the Walgrens' driveway. He scrambled out of the cab and dove for the kit in the side compartment, letting Joe DeLorme, in the passenger seat, radio dispatch that they had arrived on the scene. Cheryl Hopkins, a volunteer firefighter and EMT who was also an emergency room nurse, pulled in behind them in her own car. It had been a busy forty-eight hours treating jellyfish stings. But this call wasn't for a sting. It was for Wally Walgren, an old friend.

Wally had retired from volunteering with the fire department a number of years ago and now, in his 80s, he had a heart the doctors couldn't keep patched up. His lungs kept filling with fluid so he couldn't breathe and when that happened the only thing the EMTs could do was get him to the hospital as fast as they could. They had nearly lost him the last time. But this time Wally waved and shouted not to hurry.

He was lying in the dry, brown grass of his front yard, his wheeled walker sprawled next to him. A bed pillow cushioned his head. In the last few months his strength had failed to the point where he couldn't get up if he fell.

Irmalene, his tiny, frail wife, sat beside him on the grass. Plastic oxygen tubes hooked around his ears and looped across the grass to a small green portable tank.

"Thank you, thank you for coming," Irmalene said, patting Wally's hand. "He's okay, I just couldn't get him up."

Cheryl kneeled in the grass, listened as she pressed her stethoscope to his chest, then wrapped a blood pressure cuff around his arm.

"He couldn't breathe too good, so I got the oxygen for him," Irmalene said.

"She's my angel." Wally smiled. "You too," he said to Cheryl.

He looked around at Mick and Joe and the other firemen, neighbors who had dropped what they were doing and had driven to his house after hearing the call, ready and willing to do whatever was needed to help him.

"I've got a lot of angels—and I need 'em too, the way I drive." He grinned as he waved his hand at the walker.

"What did you do?" Mick said. "Were you trying to do skateboard tricks with that thing again?"

Wally rumbled out a laugh that degenerated into a long, wet spasm of coughing.

"I need more practice, I guess," he said when he had caught his breath. "Snagged a wheel on the edge of the ramp there and the damned thing pitched off. Nothing broken though."

"You look okay, Wally," Cheryl said as she rolled up the blood pressure cuff. "You sure nothing hurts?"

"Nah. The only thing that's injured is my dignity and I don't have much of that left anymore."

They gently moved him inside and settled him in his Lazy Boy recliner. Cheryl listened to his heart and lungs again and checked his blood pressure.

As usual, Irmalene wanted to make lemonade for everyone. But over her protests that she was just fine, Mick insisted she sit in her easy chair and chat with them for a while. Cheryl checked Irmalene's blood pressure too, which tended to run high.

When they found out that Irmalene and Wally had been on their way out to dinner at the China Star, their usual Friday night outing, one of the firemen phoned in a take-out order for noodles and egg foo young and went to pick it up for them.

104

Cheryl and the others got back in their cars and returned to their own half-eaten dinners but Mick and Joe stayed a few minutes to talk. Wally wanted to know what was happening with the real estate development company.

"Do they want to buy that five-acre lot you have out near the park?" Mick asked him.

"Yeah. But they don't want to pay anything for it." Wally frowned as he shuffled through papers on his side table. "Here it is."

He passed the real estate offer to Mick. It was outrageously low.

"What do you think? Should I sell it to them?"

"I don't know, Wally. I don't know what to do myself."

"They're saying if the development goes in, all the property values here in Cranberry Beach are going to go up. Way up. This shack could be worth something when the time comes for our kids to inherit it."

Joe also owned a small lot on the new island and had gotten his own lowball offer. "Younger hinted that you were going to sell to them," he said to Mick.

"I haven't decided yet."

Wally looked at Mick thoughtfully. "Why not?"

The only answer he could come up with was, "It's complicated."

Back in the office at the fire station, Mick entered the last call into the log. He wrote the date and time and then the spare, concise log entry. Patient assist. Walgren. Fall, no injuries. Patient left at home.

Wally Walgren had been a good friend of his father and was like an uncle to Mick. It was wrenching to see him so sick, and at times so desperate to breathe. But Wally never complained. Always happy and amiable, he deserved nothing but peace in his last years. Peace and the hope of a little prosperity.

Mick shook his head, looked back at the log and took a minute to write down the names of the volunteers who had responded.

Oakley wasn't one of them. He hadn't seen Oakley since before Sean died.

After the brief paperwork was done and the rescue truck put to rights, there wasn't much left for Mick to do. For the last couple of days he had been incredibly busy, too busy to think much about Sean, running between work at the Mercantile and first aid calls.

Newspapers and TV stations reported that thousands of the tropical jellyfish were washing ashore all along the Washington and Oregon coasts. Even though warned to stay away, a lot of curious people flocked to the beach to see them. Locally, the Sheriff's department had posted warning signs every fifty feet along the beach and patrolled it constantly in their cars. They carried epinephrine injectors for the direst cases, but called the Cranberry Beach Fire Department for emergency treatment of all reported stings—twenty-two in all, one a serious allergic reaction that had required a MedEvac helicopter transport to Seattle. Now it seemed people had finally gotten the idea that it really was dangerous to wade in even the shallowest water.

Emergency response calls had slowed down and Mick thought he would have time to go over to the Walgrens' the next day with some salvaged two-by-fours and make a handrail along the ramp to their porch. That would at least keep Wally from falling off again. He could get Sean to help.

No. Sean was gone. He kept forgetting that enormous fact.

Taking Sean's fireman's helmet from its place on the row of wall hooks, grief rose up in Mick like a bleeding wound. He took the helmet to the work bench in the back room and scraped off the reflective letters: S. Mahoney. The kid had been a volunteer firefighter since he was just barely old enough to drive a fire truck. He had wanted so much to learn, to belong, to grow up. What the hell had happened to him?

Mick rummaged around, found some acetone, and used it to rub away the remaining adhesive from the letters. Barely able to see through a flood of tears, he sprayed the helmet with cleaning solution and wiped it with a soft cloth, inside and out, working grime out of every crevice.

A knuckle rap on the open door to the workroom startled him. He brushed at the tears on his cheeks and turned to see Oakley standing in the doorway.

"Oh, hell . . . I'm sorry, Mick," Oakley said, casting his eyes around to find something other than Mick to look at.

"Just cleaning," Mick said. He took a handkerchief out of his pocket, turned away from Oakley, daubed under his glasses and blew his nose.

"Uh, Mick, I . . ." Oakley swallowed hard and looked away. "I just want to say how sorry I am about . . . everything . . . Sean . . . you know."

Oakley looked pale, anxious, fidgety. He jingled the keys in his pocket.

"Thanks, Jim." Any more talking about it would launch Mick into tears again. He worked hard to turn his thoughts to more mundane things.

He slid the helmet into an open space on the shelf over the workbench. "Went out to Walgrens' again, did you hear the call?"

"No, I—uh—was over at Spencer's Landing. Meeting. Wally okay?"

"Yeah. They're both doing okay." Mick folded the cleaning cloth and put it away under the bench. He glanced at Oakley. "Haven't seen you for a while."

Oakley, both hands in the pockets of his slacks, looked at a little broken place in the concrete of the floor, brushed at it with his toe. "I was out of town, down to L.A. actually. Business. Should have told you." He took his hands out of his pockets and tugged on the band of his expensive watch. "Sean . . . I mean, it must have been terrible for you."

It seemed like Oakley was being uncharacteristically sympathetic, which bothered Mick. He turned to look out the window so as not to have to look at Oakley.

Behind him Oakley said, "It's a shame how the kids get into drugs and crime and such."

A flush of anger crawled up Mick's throat. "I don't think that's how it was." He turned to frown at Oakley who avoided his gaze.

"Sorry, man. It's what the Sheriff was saying. I assumed you thought the same."

"No. Sean made a mistake and he paid for it. He was done with all that."

"Then . . . what do you think happened to him?"

"I don't know."

"Are there any other explanations? Any leads?"

"Not that I know of. Grayson's waiting for the toxicology report before he does anything else."

Oakley's lower lip relaxed and he almost smiled.

"Well, hell, Mick. It sucks. The whole shitty thing. Sean. Your land. All coming at the same time." He leaned against the doorjamb, hands back in his pockets.

"Thanks." Oakley's condolences had gone on too long.

"But one bright side though. SeaMist. What a lucky break for us. Lucky for you most of all. I heard what they offered you."

"I might not sell."

"What?" Oakley's face went slack with disbelief.

"I want to explore all my options."

"What other fucking options do you have?"

Mick hadn't been able to think of any, other than to wait for some undetermined amount of time for some inconceivable thing that might or might not happen.

"I'm working on it."

"But this project SeaMist is going to do—it's the best thing that ever happened to Cranberry Beach. A first class resort. Shit man, its *money*. Tourist dollars for everyone. Jobs for everyone. Jesus, Mick. There's going to be a golf course. And an airstrip. Condos, a fancy restaurant."

Mick shook his head. "Younger said it was something they were thinking about for some time in the future. It might not even happen."

"Oh, it's going to happen—soon. As soon as they can buy up the land. SeaMist is taking advantage of a rare opportunity here. A whole island. How many of those do you think are available so close to two major international airports?"

"What do you get out of it?"

Oakley grinned, spreading his arms to encompass the whole thing. "I build it."

"All this has been planned in what—five weeks since the storm?"

"Yeah," Oakley said, smiling richly.

In the back of Mick's mind something seemed like it wasn't adding up.

"You've been working for SeaMist for a long time," he said.

Oakley blinked, hesitated. "What makes you think that?"

"They own the dune cottages—and your house."

"What difference does that make? And how do you know that?"

"It's a matter of public record."

Oakley shrugged. "Regardless. Just sell your land to SeaMist. I guarantee you the best job you've ever had."

"I don't know."

"Don't be stupid, Mick. You'd be smart to accept the offer right now. Otherwise you're going to end up with nothing."

"What the hell are you talking about?"

"The holder of your mortgage is quite willing to foreclose and sell to SeaMist."

Mick didn't like the feeling of being squeezed. "I can hold out a few more months."

"Hold out for what? More money? No chance." Oakley's stare was belligerent. "If you don't sell now you have no future on the peninsula."

"What?" The sharp, cold edge in Oakley's voice put Mick on guard.

"Guy named Sam Wilson, friend of mine. Name ring a bell?"

Something stirred in Mick's memory.

"1969," Oakley drawled. "Long Beach. The Ericson. Sammy was dishonorably discharged. Just like you."

Oh yeah. Mick remembered Sammy. Shame and guilt sat down heavily on his chest. So this was how blackmail worked. It backed you into a corner.

"So the Cranberry Beach token veteran not only never went to Vietnam, he got kicked out of the Navy for smoking weed, lied about it at home, and passed the habit along to his son. For shit's sake, Mick. No wonder you kept it a secret. How are the good people around here going to feel about you if they find out?"

Mick couldn't think of anything to say.

"There's going to be a community meeting Tuesday night, right here in the fire station. SeaMist is going to show Cranberry Beach the blueprints for its future prosperity. And we're going to make a little ceremony of you signing the sales agreement and being the first one to hand it over to SeaMist. People have a lot of respect for you. They'll follow your lead. That's why we'd rather do it this way than foreclose on your mortgage."

Oakley smiled as he turned and walked away, leaving Mick dazed. A second later he was back in the doorway.

"And you can tell that fucking turtle bitch to butt out. She doesn't even live here."

* * *

On Saturday afternoon Mick saw Anna come into the Crow's Nest, talking with a man he didn't know. It had been a stressful day and Mick had the impulse to hide his face behind the newspaper he was reading. But curiosity about who Anna's friend could be overcame his desire for a solitary cup of coffee. He waved them over.

He had seen Anna earlier that day in Astoria at the memorial service Julie had arranged for Sean. Anna had left before the coffee and cookie reception was over. He hadn't talked with her, but had wordlessly accepted her sympathetic hand-squeeze.

Now, scooting into the booth across from him, Anna was kind enough not to bring up the memorial service. Her companion slid a laptop computer onto the table and eased into the seat beside Anna.

"Mick, this is the coworker I told you about, my friend Maury Quinn from National Marine Fisheries in Newport." Mick reached across the table to shake Maury's hand. He was a big man, firmly muscled, about Mick's age but in better shape. Maury's hair was still dark and only slightly receding. Anna and Maury touched each other as they talked, squeezing a forearm for emphasis, patting a hand, leaning companionably shoulder to shoulder. They were obviously comfortable old friends.

After they ordered pie and coffee, Anna and Maury got to talking about the jellyfish. Mick's thoughts drifted back to the memorial service.

A lot of people had come even though Julie had insisted on having it in Astoria, a half-hour's drive from the peninsula. In a way, she had divorced herself from the whole community when she picked up and left Mick. She didn't ever want to go back. But that hadn't kept people from coming to pay their last respects to Sean.

Just about everyone from the fire department attended, except for Oakley which didn't surprise anyone. Sandy Jenkins, the same age as Sean, wept the whole time with crumpled tissues pressed to her face. She and Sean had joined the department at the same time, had learned the ropes together, had fought fires and responded to emergencies with the headlong enthusiasm of the young. After Sean's arrest, Sandy's father, a twenty-year member of the fire department, had expressed his disapproval of her friendship with Sean. But George was there at the service, his arm protectively encircling his daughter's shoulders. When he shook Mick's hand afterwards in the reception line, his eyes were red. He murmured, "Sean was a good kid. I don't believe what they're saying about him." It was a sentiment expressed by many who greeted Mick and Julie. The ones who weren't sure just said it was a great loss and they were so sorry.

More people attended than the little chapel's wooden pews could hold. They filled all the rickety folding chairs set up in the aisles and more stood in the back listening to the minister talking about Sean.

Though Mick's family had rarely entered any kind of church, the Reverend Fred Blake had agreed to Julie's request that he preside over the service. Father Blake was an Episcopal priest. His kids had gone to school with Sean.

Father Blake talked about how we never really know the whole story about anybody else, even our closest neighbors. So we can never have enough information to judge them. Only God can do that, he said, so that's one thing we don't have to be responsible for. Then he went on to list all the good things he knew about Sean. It took a long time . . .

Mick realized that Maury and Anna were looking at him as if expecting an answer.

"Sorry—what?" he said.

"Are you still getting calls for jellyfish stings?"

"Oh—not since yesterday."

"Maury thinks the bluebottles are going to drift away from shore for the next few days."

Maury stirred sugar and cream into his second cup of coffee. "The weather service is saying the wind should shift by tomorrow morning."

"What about sea surface temperature?" Anna asked. "Is it still in the seventies here?"

"Yes, temperature is holding at about twenty-five Celsius. That's at a half-mile offshore. Of course, we don't have the array of sensing buoys we had a decade ago, so the data isn't complete."

Anna glanced at Mick. "Twenty-five degrees Celsius is seventy-seven Fahrenheit. That's warm for the north Pacific—*very* warm for the first week of October."

As Maury went into a detailed explanation of something scientific, Mick's thoughts wandered back to the memorial service. He had talked with Stew Johnston as they stood around after the service eating fancy cookies and sipping tea from china cups. Sean had been staying at the Johnstons' house for the past few weeks, helping with storm repairs and clean up. Stew told Mick about the

112

statement he had given to the Sheriff's office. He had been one the last people to see Sean alive.

"We were salvaging on the beach," Stew said, "cutting up some two-by-fours for firewood and tossing the pieces into the back of Sean's pickup truck. He found something odd half-buried in the sand so he dug it up. I thought it might have been the kind of remote control device you use for flying model airplanes. But it was so mangled you couldn't really tell what it was. Sean was interested in the bit of lettering on it. It was that kind of backward-looking writing they use in Russia. He put it in the glove box of his truck and said he wanted to ask Boris Badenov about it."

"Why Boris?" An uneasy feeling tugged in Mick's stomach.

"I don't know. Nobody talks to that weirdo. Maybe he wanted to ask what the Russian writing said. Anyway, after dinner at our house Sean left in his truck. He didn't say where he was going, but that's a young man's privilege." Stew's voice wobbled. "Sean never came back."

His truck had been found in the brush near the meth trailer. The Sheriff's department had towed it from the crime scene to their garage in Spencer's Landing. They had searched it for evidence, dusted it for fingerprints and released it to Mick a few days ago. It was in the back parking lot of the Mercantile now, next to Mick's old Chevy pickup. They hadn't told him whether they found anything. He wondered if the remote control thing was still in the glove box . . .

Maury flipped open his laptop, interrupting Mick's private thoughts.

"I've got the latest data from NOAA," Maury was saying to Anna. "Downloaded it this morning."

Anna leaned close to Maury to see the computer screen as he typed.

"Huh. Look at this Mick." She turned the computer toward him.

A brilliantly colored picture filled the screen. At first all Mick could make of it was more or less horizontal layers of red, yellow and a little green. Anna tapped at the center of the picture with her finger.

"This is the north Pacific Ocean," she said. Then, touching black areas to the right and left of the picture, she said, "North America, Asia."

"Hmmm," Mick said, not really understanding what he was looking at.

"This is a picture of sea surface temperatures," Anna said. "See, here are the Aleutians and the Bering Sea. It's very warm up there, the yellow-green indicates the surface temperature of the water is about sixty degrees Fahrenheit, fifteen degrees warmer than usual. Which is incredible. And right here where we are," she pointed to the northwest corner of the United States, "The red tells us we're in the high seventies. That's water temperature, not air."

Mick studied the picture, not yet grasping the significance that Anna and Maury seemed to see in it.

"So, what does this mean?" he asked.

Anna turned the computer back around and typed something. She swung it around again to show Mick.

"This is the north Pacific ten years ago."

It was a completely different picture. Mick could see that there was a lot more blue and green in it. The area of magenta, red and orange was contained in a wide stripe that followed the equator. Yellow colored the coastal waters off North America.

"This is important. See that?" Anna pointed to a thin wedge of blue that edged between the yellow color of the sea and the coastlines of Washington, Oregon and the northern part of California. She turned the computer around and made a few keystrokes that returned the first picture she had shown him. The thin blue wedge was gone now and most of the north Pacific was orange or red, right up to the edge of the land.

"You don't have to *believe* in global warming. Here it is," she said. "And it's happening fast."

"There are some indications that the California current might be turning off," Maury said. He looked seriously concerned.

Anna showed Mick the ten-year-old picture again and pointed to the blue offshore wedge. "This is where the cold ocean current flows along the northwest coast from north to south." She

114

flipped again to the current picture. "It's not keeping the warm water away from the coast now."

Mick tried to absorb that. "It's only temporary though. It will go back to the way it was when winter comes . . . won't it?"

Anna glanced at Maury and shrugged. "We'll have to wait and see," she said.

Maury scowled as he turned the computer off and closed the top. "There's been too much waiting already. We're shit-out-of-luck now. The politicians have had their heads in the sand about this so long that nothing humans can do will make any difference. There might have been a chance a decade ago. But not now. This is not temporary."

"What does that mean?" Mick asked.

"It means we'll all have to adjust to the changes that come, whatever those are going to be. It will be easier for some, harder for others."

"You mean we'll have to be closing the beaches every time the wind blows?"

"Maybe."

"A lot of species, especially those that live on the land, are going to die out," Anna said. "The bluebottles sail with the wind and as long as the water's warm they can survive. It's the species that can't move with their changing habitats that are going to face extinction."

"What about your turtles?"

Anna smiled. "It's warm enough for them now in these waters and on this beach. And the great thing about the bluebottles is . . ." She grinned as she paused for dramatic effect. "They're turtle food."

9

Mick walked the two blocks back to the Mercantile, leaving Anna and Maury to their scientific talk in the Crow's Nest. The idea of global warming was confusing—too enormous and complicated to absorb. No wonder the politicians ignored it.

He tried to think through his own confusing mess of problems. Oakley's blackmail was detestable, but that aside, maybe the resort *would* be good for the peninsula. Nearly half of the peninsula's population was unemployed and had been for too long. Most of the others labored occasionally at odd jobs, picking up a few bucks here and there, digging the septic systems made necessary by the storm and replacing wind-damaged roofs. But those jobs wouldn't last long, and after that—what?

A few people were trying subsistence farming out on the island, but with transportation issues and no electric power, it was turning out to be more work than it was worth. Things were different now from pioneer times. His great-grandfather had homesteaded before there was even a road on the peninsula. He had rowed across the bay in a boat loaded with tools, seed, and his wife's Baltimore china dishes. He hacked an opening in the forest, built a cabin, planted a garden, fished and hunted and raised his family. But now it took electricity and the internet and a phone and insurance and a freezer and a car and a university degree to build a life. And a mortgage. All bought with money--the scarcest resource on the peninsula.

If he led the way by being the first to sell to SeaMist, he could be doing a good thing for his neighbors and friends, something to redeem his deception. Then maybe it wouldn't ever be necessary to expose his secret. Maybe things would go along just fine without ever having to do that. But does blackmail ever end?

He detoured around the back of the Mercantile and climbed into Sean's pickup. A wave of grief washed over him.

Sean had been a tidy person. He had never allowed the accumulation of hamburger wrappers, empty pop cans, and other miscellaneous items that littered so many young men's vehicles. Under the passenger seat Mick found a tool box and a neatly coiled rope. A fire extinguisher was mounted to a panel behind the seat and he had stowed a fishing tackle box under the driver's seat next to three emergency flares in a shallow box. The rack across the back window held a fishing rod and reel.

Black dust smudged the steering wheel, dashboard, door panels and handles, remains of the fingerprint investigation. The technicians hadn't cleaned up after themselves.

With the heel of his hand, Mick brushed the dark smudges off the latch of the glove box. Inside he found a map of Washington and Oregon, registration papers and proof of insurance for the truck. Mick smiled at the package of condoms tucked into a back corner. A man needs to be ready if the opportunity arises. He didn't think Sean had a girlfriend, though judging by her tears at the memorial service, maybe Sandy had been.

There was a sprinkle of sand in the glove box but no broken remote control device with backward writing. Cyrillic was the word for that alphabet, Mick remembered. Russian. Maybe the investigators had taken it.

That Sean should connect the device with Boris was natural since he was the only purported Russian in the vicinity. It could have belonged to him, though it was hard to picture Boris with a model airplane hobby. The device could just as well have fallen off a Russian trawler and washed ashore with the mounds of foreign and domestic garbage that drifted onto the beaches every day. But it was odd that Sean would want to approach the prickly Russian with something that only amounted to idle curiosity. Mick made a mental note to ask Sheriff Grayson if Boris had been contacted in the investigation. Maybe he could shed some light on Sean's last hours.

117

* * *

At 10:25 the next morning the Cranberry Beach Fire Department responded to a single vehicle accident five miles south of town. Arriving on the scene in the pumper truck, Mick saw the swath of broken saplings and crushed blackberry canes that marked the car's careening path through the brush. Bob Simpson, a volunteer firefighter, happened to have been following the blue hatch-back as it alternated swaying across the center line and swiping the graveled shoulder at twice the recommended speed for the county road. He had followed at a safe distance until the small car over-corrected after a curve, hurtled off the road to the right and slammed into an alder tree about fifty feet away. The tree cracked from the impact and the top half fell onto the roof of the car. Bob had used his cell phone to call for assistance as he plunged through the brush to see if there were any survivors.

Now, as he led Mick and three other firefighters back to the crash site, Bob filled them in on the condition of the driver.

"Drunk as a skunk—on Sunday morning, for God's sake," he grumbled as thorns stabbed through the fabric of his jeans. His feet, covered only by sandals, were scratched and bleeding and blotched with the purple juice of crushed blackberries.

Mick and the others strode through the brambles, protected by their heavy turnout gear and boots. Sandy Jenkins, who had driven the rescue truck, carried the jump kit.

"Is she conscious?" Mick asked.

"Hell, yes," Bob answered. "And I don't see much blood either which is damned amazing when you see the car."

A woman yelled from up ahead in the brush. "Hello—hello—could somebody please help me?"

"That's her," Bob said.

"I'm stuu . . . . uuuk," she sang, drawing out the syllables into a little three-note song.

The firefighters glanced at each other and grinned.

118

The front of the car had folded like an accordion, jamming both doors shut. Mick bent to look through the open window on the driver's side. The crumpled dashboard sat firmly on the driver's legs. The steering wheel pressed into her chest, pinning her tightly against the seat back which remained upright with the headrest supporting her neck. The crushed roof pressed down on her blonde, frizzy head, preventing her from turning it in any direction. She had several cuts and scratches on her face, arms and hands, probably from flying glass. The windshield was gone.

Airbags hadn't been a feature of this older model car but safety didn't seem a high priority for the lone occupant. She wasn't wearing her seatbelt.

She pressed upward on the ceiling with her hands, straining mightily to try to lift it away.

"Get this off of me, will you?" she growled through clenched teeth.

She wore skimpy red shorts. Below her sports bra, Mick saw a snake tattoo curving around her ribcage.

"Hi, Meredith," he said.

She stretched her eyes sideways to look at him and giggled. "Have we met?"

"Yes. When you got your broken ribs—at the trailer, remember?"

"Oh yeah. Yeah. That time. Fonzie can be such a shit. But thank you." Her eyes darted continuously and her fingers drummed on the steering wheel. "Appreciate it. Really do. Really."

Mick interrupted. "Meredith, we're going to get you out of there. But we've got to take our time and do it right, okay?"

"Well, okay. No, I don't really have time. Can you do it quickly? I'm late. Gotta go now." She pushed the ceiling again, grunting with the effort.

"Meredith, there's no way you can push that roof up. There's a tree on it. But we're going to get it off. You just have to stay calm and let us do our job."

Mick pried her left hand off the ceiling and pressed two fingers to the pulse in her wrist. It was racing but strong.

"You've got to calm down, Meredith. Take a few deep breaths while I check you out."

He took off his helmet and coat to make himself small enough to lean in through the open window and look around. DeLorme had pushed through the blackberries to the passenger side and leaned in through that window. He shook his head to indicate to Mick that he saw nothing alarming.

Meredith was tightly pinned but Mick saw no pools of blood seeping under the seat or the dash. He felt around the far side of her face and explored her head through the frizzy blonde hair and found no blood there either. Amazing.

She took one deep breath, held it, then blew it out in an expletive. "Fuck. I can't be calm. I'm late. Gotta go. Gotta get on the road. I'll be calm later. When it wears off."

"Do you feel pain anywhere Meredith?" He didn't smell alcohol on her breath.

"Not really. No. Well, just a little. My knees. OH GOD MY KNEES! I can't move them. I can't move my feet."

"We'll get you out, just hang in there."

He squeezed Meredith's hand and straightened up to call out to Sandy. "Go to the truck and get the big chainsaw first. Then go back and bring the Jaws."

Sandy nodded and bounded back through the brush to where the firetruck was parked on the road.

Mick stuck his head through the window again and stretched to see into the back seat. There was enough room to release the seat back and lower it, to relieve the pressure from the steering wheel on Meredith's chest and to ease her head away from the roof. But the driver side door was jammed. Before they could reach the seat latch and extricate her they would have to cut the driver's side door off.

Meredith babbled nonstop into his ear. On the floor of the back seat Mick saw what was probably the source of her intoxication. Spilled from a large, pink, raffia beach bag, several small plastic packets of a crystalline substance lay scattered on the floor with a glass pipe and two syringes.

120

He backed out of the window and squatted beside the door. "Meredith, Meredith!" He got her to stop talking. "You said 'when it wears off.' What are you on—meth?"

Meredith bit her lip. She looked sideways and her eyes teared up. "Oh, don't be mad at me. Please don't be mad at me."

"I'm not mad at you. But we have to know so we can help you."

"Well . . . well. I . . . uh . . . no, I don't have any meth. No. I'm just excited because of this wreck. Nervous. You know? Anybody would be. Stuck like this."

Her pupils were large and black.

"Okay. You don't have to tell us. You can tell the people in the emergency room. We'll get you out no matter what you're on."

Mick felt a tap on his shoulder and turned to see Deputy Rick Harmon behind him.

"Let me talk to her for a minute," Harmon said.

Meredith's eyes slid sideways to look at the deputy then squeezed tightly shut.

Mick stood up to let Harmon kneel by the window.

"Meredith," Harmon said. "We can see your stash on the floor back there. Are you making deliveries today?"

"Oh fuck. Oh shit."

"It'll go a lot better for you if you cooperate."

"How can I cooperate when I'm stuck in here? I can't even defend myself!"

She started pushing on the ceiling again.

"Just tell us where your cousin . . . or whatever . . . is. Where's Fonzie? We just want to talk to him."

"Fonzie bugged out. He left. Freaked out. Don't know where."

"When did you see him last?"

"After . . . oh shit, I'm STUCK here." She pounded on the ceiling. "Just GET ME OUT OF HERE!"

Meredith let out a howl and beat frantically on the steering wheel.

Mick touched Harmon's shoulder. "She's losing her cool. You can talk to her at the hospital. It's better for everyone if she's as calm as possible during the extrication."

Harmon nodded and backed off a few feet. Sandy arrived, carrying the chainsaw. Two newly arrived firefighters followed with the Jaws of Life apparatus. Sandy's dad brought up the rear with the Stokes stretcher and backboard. When all the people and gear pushed up close to the wrecked car there was no place for Harmon to stand except in the blackberry brambles.

Mick thought maybe the deputy felt like he needed to stay close in case the suspect tried to escape. Considering Meredith's jacked up condition there was a possibility of that. And Harmon might come in handy if they needed more muscle during the extrication.

"Anybody else show up?" Mick asked Sandy.

"Just Hermie and my dad. Oh, and Oakley stopped by."

Mick looked in the direction of the road. "Is he coming back in here?"

"Uh—I don't think so." Sandy frowned, hesitated, then spoke her mind. "Why doesn't he *participate* in calls? I mean, isn't he supposed to be our leader?"

Everyone took a break from their tasks to glance at Mick.

"Not the time for that discussion," Mick said, more gruffly than he intended. "Right now we're helping this lady get out of her smashed car."

Mick leaned in the window to thread a cervical collar between the headrest and Meredith's neck. She objected vehemently as he fastened it under her chin.

"This is just to make sure we don't hurt you any more when we move you out of here," Mick said, wincing from the stabbing noise of her shrieks.

He backed out of the window, stood up and studied the way the tree trunk lay across the car. It could be safely cut and pushed away. He directed Hornsby, the most experienced one with a chainsaw, to make the cut.

Though Mick had explained to Meredith what they were going to do, she screamed the whole time the chainsaw was biting through the tree. Afterwards, sobbing, she told him she had thought they were sawing through the roof of the car.

He got her calmed down to the point of babbling again, and turned his attention to the process they would go through to extricate her. She was relatively uninjured, just wedged in.

"Okay," Mick said. "This lady is stable and we're not in a hurry. So this is a good chance for Sandy and Hermie to get some experience."

Sandy nodded, grinned, and went for the box of extrication gear. Hermie, who had just turned eighteen, held back a second, wide-eyed.

Mick didn't want to give Hermie a pep talk where Meredith might hear and come to the conclusion that her rescuers were incompetent. So he pointed at the gas engine of the Jaws apparatus and gave Hermie a direct order.

"Get the power unit started up, Paterson."

That was something Hermie knew how to do. As the portable gas engine putted out blue exhaust, Sandy and Hermie, with occasional instructions from the three older firefighters, assembled the hoses that would power the hydraulic Jaws of Life.

Mick leaned on the window frame to talk to Meredith.

"Now we're going to get you out, one step at a time."

"Okay. I won't cry this time. Just *explain* everything first."

"Right. The first thing we're going to do is cut and bend this door off."

George handed Mick a thick blanket and said to Meredith, "We're going to put this blanket over you in case any glass flies around. To keep you safe."

Meredith flailed her arms, pushing the blanket away.

"You've got to keep those arms still, Meredith. Out of the way," Mick said.

"No. I can't do it. Don't cover me up." She flapped her hands at the blanket.

Mick straightened up. "Okay, cut here, here, and here," he said to Sandy and Hermie, pointing to places on the door posts. "George, show these two what to do."

Mick pushed his way through the blackberries to the passenger side and leaned as far as he could through the open window. DeLorme passed two corners of the blanket to Mick through the other window. Together they wrestled it around Meredith's head and what they could reach of the rest of her body, wrapping it around behind the seat back.

Mick held the blanket tight to pin her arms. Her protests turned panicky and breathless.

"Everything's okay, Meredith," Mick said. "Just breathe slowly now. You're hyperventilating. They're cutting through the door now with what amounts to a very big pair of tin snips."

"Oh shit. Oh shit. Oh shit," she gasped.

After the cuts were made they switched to the spreader tool and in less than a minute pried the door open.

"I'm going to break this back window glass," George called out.

Mick tightened his grip on the blanket and turned his face away to shield it from the shower of safety glass. With a heavy crescent wrench George whittled away the remaining rim of shattered glass. Then he leaned in to support the back of the seat while DeLorme released the seat latch. They slowly lowered the seat to a half-reclining position, freeing Meredith from the bent roof and the steering wheel.

"Is that better?" Mick asked over her sobs.

"Yes. Better. But my knees are still stuck," she wailed.

"Just hold still. Don't turn your head, Meredith. We need to keep your neck still in case it's hurt."

She did turn it, blinking at Mick with tear-filled eyes.

"I wish I hadn't done that second hit," she said.

"It didn't improve your driving," Mick said, smiling.

She smiled in return. "No, but I was getting a *lot* done."

Her expression sobered and she teared up again. "I haven't slept or eaten in three days." Her mouth trembled and pulled down

124

into a grimace revealing black stubs of teeth. "And I don't feel well. This stuff of Fonzie's is *shit*."

"What stuff? What did you take?"

"Fonzie's secret recipe. He says he invented it himself. It's just a different variation."

"Of meth?"

"Yeah."

George was showing Sandy and Hermie how to position the ram against the dash.

"Okay, Meredith, they're getting ready to lift the dash off your knees. It'll go slowly, so you just have to be patient and calm. You can talk to me to pass the time."

He smiled to reassure her as he renewed his grasp on the blanket. His back and shoulders ached from the strain of leaning in through the window.

"Ooooooh," Meredith wailed. "What's that noise?"

"They've switched on the ram. In a couple seconds the dash will start lifting up."

"Fonzie's going to kick my ass. This is his car. And what I didn't wreck, you people are finishing off."

"But you said Fonzie's gone."

"Not *gone*. He's at the other place. The place nobody knows about."

It wasn't Mick's job to get information in criminal investigations. And it was highly inappropriate, even for Deputy Harmon, to question a victim before she had even been extricated from a car crash. But as long as she was talking . . .

"So he bugged out after the—incident—a couple weeks ago?" Mick asked.

"Incident? Oh, yeah, the dead guy in the driveway."

Something cracked in the car's chassis, making Meredith cry out.

"That's okay. Nothing to worry about. The ram's moving the dash up now."

Meredith started talking again. "The crazy thing about that dead guy is we didn't know him. At all. Never saw him before.

Fonzie went outside that morning to take a leak in the woods like he always does. He likes to do that, the damned pervert. Anyway, he sees this pickup truck parked there and this dead body and he's like, what the hell? And he thinks he hears a siren far away, you know, and he thinks the cops are coming. So he grabs some of his precious ingredients and we bug out. The back way, through the brush."

"So you didn't know the—dead guy. Or how he got there."

"Complete mystery."

Mick felt a whisper of hope.

"Sean Mahoney," he said. "Ever hear that name?"

"No." Meredith gazed at him, dry-eyed now. "Is that the name of the dead guy?"

"Yeah. Do you know most of the drug dealers around here?"

"We *are* the local drug dealers," she giggled, and in a cartoon voice squeaked, "Oops, I shouldn't have said that. Where's that damned deputy anyway?"

Mick smiled. "He's over on the other side. He can't hear you over the power unit."

She smiled back. "My ass is grass anyway. Big time. But no, I don't know that name. And I would if he was doing business around here."

"What about marijuana? Would you know if he was selling that?"

Meredith rolled her eyes. "There's a store for that in Astoria. And besides, nobody wants that here. Only kids and old people—like you—want it." She grinned.

Mick felt a pang of guilt.

"Our customers need energy for getting things done. They want to lose weight. They want to *speed up*, not slow down. They don't want to be all soft and mellow like weed gets you. They don't want *the munchies* for shit's sake."

The ram finished lifting the dash off Meredith's bare legs. Big dents across her shins suggested broken bones and blood oozed from patches of scraped skin. But it could have been so much worse.

"Okay, we're going to transfer you to the stretcher now."

Meredith panicked again. "No—no—no! I can't move!"

"Just relax. We're going to move you. You don't have to do anything."

"I can't feel my LEGS!"

Mick released his grip on the blanket as the other firefighters maneuvered the backboard under Meredith. She thrashed her arms and screamed as they lifted her up over the ram and lowered her into the stretcher. Mick worked his way around the car.

"Let's get her buckled up and into the rescue truck," he said.

Sandy held Meredith's flailing arms down while George fastened the straps over them.

"I could cuff her if you want," Harmon suggested.

"She's secure this way," Mick said. "Are you arresting her?"

The deputy took a card from his pocket and commenced reading the Miranda recitation but it was doubtful Meredith heard it over her cursing and wailing.

Following the stretcher back to the road, Mick felt relief and elation. He had believed in Sean's innocence and now there was a concrete, specific clue for the Sheriff's office to investigate. What Meredith had said about not knowing Sean was going to change everything in the investigation of his murder.

10

On Tuesday evening, a crew of volunteers rolled the two fire trucks and the rescue truck out of the fire station and set up rows of folding chairs in preparation for SeaMist's community meeting. They were expecting a big crowd. Mick leaned against the wall behind the chairs watching Marvin Younger and a pretty young assistant fuss over the cables of a big screen TV.

He spotted Sheriff Grayson coming through the side door. Mick wanted to talk to him. The sheriff hadn't returned his calls after Meredith's wreck so Mick had left the information in a voice mail message. He hadn't gotten an answer to that yet either.

He caught up with Grayson who was glad-handing his way through the crowd of arriving people, schmoozing up votes for re-election.

"Mick, how ya doin?" The sheriff's meaty hand was sweaty and moisture ringed the shirt collar of his dress uniform where the neck fat rolled over it.

"Did you get my message?" Mick asked.

"What message?" Grayson's eyes roved the room, looking for voters.

Mick was starting to get ticked off. "About what Meredith— the woman from that meth trailer—said about Sean."

Grayson frowned. "Oh. Yeah. You said she told you she didn't know him."

"Well? Did somebody talk to her about it?"

"Meredith has clammed up. She just wants to stay in jail, away from that shit Fonzie. She's afraid of him. Refuses to say anything to anybody."

"But she said it to me. Isn't that convincing enough to investigate?"

The sheriff's jaw tightened. "From what I understand, she was high as a kite when she said that. And besides, I don't have the personnel to work the case. I've had to lay off several deputies and staff because my friggin' budget's been axed again."

He pasted on a smile for someone across the room. "I've got to talk to that guy."

"But what about Boris Badenov? Did you contact him?"

"Who? Shit, Mick. Did you hear what I was just saying?"

Jim Oakley interrupted them, giving the sheriff a good-old-boy slap on the back. He pumped Mick's hand, grinning expansively.

Mick was speechless. Oakley had dressed up in a formal fire chief's uniform complete with fancy braid on the cuffs and a naval officer style hat with fire department insignia, gold braid and oak leaves on the bill. His necktie was fastened with a tie bar decorated with an American eagle on crossed fire hose nozzles. The Cranberry Beach Volunteer Fire Department had never seen anything like it. It was ridiculous, pompous, an eyesore. But visually it put Oakley on a par with the sheriff who always wore his dress uniform to public gatherings.

Sandy, George and Frank stood snickering near the door. Sandy caught Mick's eye, indicated the chief with a tilt of her head, and grinned.

The sheriff resumed hand-shaking his way across the room. Oakley stood beside Mick with folded arms, surveying the crowd of peninsula residents.

"Good turnout," he said.

"What the hell kind of get-up is that?" Mick said in a lowered voice, glancing at Oakley.

Not only was the outfit ostentatious, it was obviously too warm. Sweat trickled down Oakley's temples. He straightened his tie and pretended to brush specks off his sleeve. "I look pretty sharp."

"The hell you do. You look like an asshole."

"It doesn't matter what *you* think," Oakley said evenly. "The only thing that matters about you is that you're going to be the first to sign your land over to SeaMist."

Mick didn't answer. A flush of anger was making the notch in his ear burn.

"Okay, if that's the way you want it," Oakley said. "We can get it from Puget Sound Fidelity. So either way we've got it. It's just that it would be a lot nicer if you lead the way. That way *everyone wins* including you. The other way, you get no money and you lose the respect of everyone you know."

"Frankly, Jim, I can't picture you getting up there and telling tales about me."

"Oh, no. I wouldn't do it that way. Gossip is much better. Just start the grapevine. News travels fast in a podunk place like this. Everyone would know about your dishonorable lying ass by tomorrow morning."

Oakley gave him a mocking smile and winked as he walked away.

Mick resisted the impulse to go after Oakley, grab his asinine tie, and twist it until he choked.

He stood in the back of the room, letting his blood pressure return to normal. The hall was buoyant with anticipation as a dozen small children orbited round the room squealing in general excitement. He watched Wally shuffle in pushing his walker, Irmalene beside him carrying his portable oxygen bottle. They took seats in the front row next to Bev who was talking with Jimmy Whittaker's parents. Nearly everyone he saw was a friend and neighbor. Most of them had lived poor all their lives, stitching up a patchwork of odd jobs, minimum wages, cash under the table and state assistance.

Prosperity was something they all wished for and this resort development looked like the answer to their dreams. Maybe it was the best thing for the community and the easiest solution for himself. But he respected Anna's intelligence and her skepticism worried him.

Right now he wasn't sure which way he would go when the time came to sign the sales offer.

Anna arrived late carrying several bags and cases, accompanied by Loretta Primrose, the town librarian. Loretta's cropped gray hair stuck out in frenzied licks and her face glowed red with the heat and physical exertion. Anna was flushed too.

They dashed into the kitchenette and came out carrying a small table past Winnie Nelson, the mayor, who had just stood up and raised her right arm, index finger extended toward the ceiling. This was Winnie's way of getting people's attention, something she had done as a grade school teacher. She never raised her voice. Gradually, as people noticed what Winnie was doing, they ended their conversations, quieted and raised their own hands. Soon a forest of fingers pointed to the ceiling.

In the back of the room Anna and Loretta could be heard whispering, unzipping bags and clicking latches. People turned around to see what was going on.

Winnie kept her hand up. She never settled for less than complete attention and everyone knew it. But Anna and Loretta were busy and they didn't look up.

Mick, under the bemused looks of about a hundred of his neighbors, went over and whispered to Anna, "Prayer time."

The two women stopped bustling and stood quietly as Winnie, a fervent Baptist, prayed long and hard for the success of the meeting. She always prayed before any meeting. Most people appreciated it. Even Mick usually found it a good time to settle in and focus on the agenda.

All the seats were filled and a few stood around behind the chairs. It looked like all of the people who owned land on the new island were there as well as most of the others who lived on the peninsula.

Benny sprawled on the cool concrete floor, panting under the small table Anna and Loretta had brought from the kitchen. On it a laptop computer sat open next to a projector. It looked like they would be offering information of their own to the meeting. Anna stood quietly with her eyes closed. She wore her usual outfit of blue jeans, cotton shirt and sandals and her long gray hair was pulled back in a ponytail. Sweat beaded her forehead and upper lip. Prayer time had halted Loretta in the process of plugging in a long, orange extension cord. She stood at attention, sweat running in rivers down her face, her wrinkled Bermuda shorts hiked up on her pudgy thighs.

Loretta's offhand comment about Mick's mortgage had proved chillingly true, though he was sure she never intended anything prophetic. She just knew things. Not only facts gleaned from reading anything that came her way. She was a good thinker too.

The prayer ended with a hearty "Amen" from the people. Winnie had covered the reasons for the meeting copiously in her prayer, reminding God of the disaster that had almost been the last straw for the struggling community after so many years of unemployment and growing poverty. And she praised God for sending SeaMist to solve all their problems. So the only other thing she had to do was introduce Marvin Younger.

He wasn't wearing his suit. He was wearing what Mick thought must be business casual, a pale yellow polo shirt made of something a lot more expensive than cotton with the SeaMist wave logo embroidered on the left chest. His khaki slacks were perfectly pressed and worn with a brown leather belt and topsider shoes. The navy sports jacket hung on a chair. Unlike Oakley, Younger had the sense to take off his jacket. His girl assistant had on the same outfit.

Younger adjusted the tiny microphone on his headset. "Good evening, Cranberry Beach," he said. "Can everyone hear me?"

No one complained.

On the wall behind Younger a huge poster of the SeaMist logo reminded Mick of the wave on the peninsula's tsunami warning signs. On either side of it they had taped up posters of the site plan for the new development and an artist's rendition of its golf course and condominiums. They had put a lot of work into planning in an incredibly short amount of time. It was clear SeaMist wanted this project a lot. Mick hoped his neighbors would understand that they had some room for negotiation.

SeaMist, Younger announced, was thrilled to have the opportunity to team up with the community in a joint effort that would pay off generously for everyone. He spoke with an infectious, confident enthusiasm. In a few minutes he had his audience smiling.

"But everyone knows a picture is worth a thousand words," he said. "So we invite you to sit back and enjoy this video presentation."

The assistant used a remote to start the DVD and adjust the sound level. Oakley cut the room lights.

"Welcome to Cranberry Beach, SeaMist's newest four-star resort," the voiceover proclaimed. A rapid succession of images pictured a village of quaintly decorated shops. Cranberries carried the theme in every possible way: Jars of cranberry preserves topped with ruffled gingham and bows, sweatshirts, T-shirts and socks appliqued with cranberry designs, a woman beaming with pride, offering cranberry pie in a country-style restaurant.

The pictures followed tourists as they tromped along boardwalks through marshy trails. One shot zoomed in close on someone standing in a bog in hip boots fingering ripe, red cranberries. There were some local long distance shots over the bay toward the hills and a sunset view of the ocean beach. But most of the pictures had been taken somewhere else, probably on the east coast. It could have been Cape Cod.

The video switched to an aerial view out the windows of a small plane coming in for a landing on a paved runway. A manicured golf course spread out to the left, its impossibly green grass pocked with contrived-looking water features and sand traps. A groundskeeper operating a riding lawnmower waved up at the airplane. It was nothing but a damned theme park for rich people.

Landscaped groupings of expensive homes clustered along the ocean to the right. Condos and hotels crowded the edge of a beach polka dotted with sun umbrellas and lounge chairs. The plane landed, people got out. Respectful, uniformed staff greeted them and collected their luggage.

Interior shots showed elegant hotel rooms. Windows looked out over private decks to ocean views. A beautiful woman enjoyed a professional massage in a candlelit spa. A man lifted weights in a gym.

The scene shifted to a couple walking on the beach in yellow rain slickers. Wind tossed their hair as they romped exuberantly in the wave wash of a stormy surf. Mick shook his head. Another storm like the last one would wipe that resort out in a few hours.

Later the couple snuggled in their private Jacuzzi sipping glasses of wine in front of a crackling fire. A perfect destination for a winter retreat.

The video turned to a study of architects' plans. The narrator described the orientation of homes and hotels along the ocean side of the island. It was going to be a village. In addition to the superb golf course there would be a world-class restaurant, a movie theater, a game lounge, and three swimming pools. A system of paved bicycle trails would web the island. A marina suitable for ocean-going yachts was planned for the bay side.

The plans showed a road on a rock dike connecting the island with the mainland. It crossed the three-quarters of a mile of Mick's submerged land, bridging fifty feet across the deepest portion of the channel where the current flowed fastest. Mick thought it would be costly.

A causeway and bridge like that would be impossible for the island land owners to build, even if they pooled all their financial resources. There was no way to beat it. SeaMist held all the cards.

As the narrator's voice droned on, a memory of his family's ancient homestead rose in Mick's mind. The wood floors his mother had polished. The barn with its mortised beams. The garden soil, loamy from a hundred years of compost. The fruit trees and pastures, wild marshes and forests. Replaced by a prissy, exclusive, damned golf course.

SeaMist would have it, that much was clear. The only choice left to Mick was whether or not to take the money.

When the lights came back on people chattered breathlessly, no doubt speculating on how big a piece of this pie would come to them. Younger opened it up for questions.

Mayor Nelson raised her hand and waited for Younger's nod before speaking.

"I noticed you call this resort 'Cranberry Beach.' But this," she pointed at the ground, "is Cranberry Beach. Kind of confusing."

Younger smiled. "It's a great name and a great theme. We see the resort as a sort of extension of the town."

A gift store owner said, "So you want us to fix up our stores like we saw in the movie? I can't even afford a window cleaner to wash my windows."

"SeaMist will offer low-cost loans to some businesses to help with upgrading."

"Only some businesses?"

"At first only the ones that front the main road," Younger said.

"What if we don't want to do the cranberry theme?"

Younger smiled. "Cranberries are the theme SeaMist has decided on. In fact, we've planned a yearly cranberry festival during Thanksgiving weekend. It's sure to bring in a lot of tourism."

Phil Hastings, whose family had farmed cranberries on the peninsula for decades, stood up. "I don't know if you folks are aware of this," he blustered, "but we used to have the cranberry festival — in October. But we don't anymore because, well, we don't grow cranberries. Cranberry Beach doesn't *have* cranberries."

"No problem." Younger put his hand up in a reassuring gesture. "We have plans for a demonstration bog on the island. And we'll ship in all the cranberry products we need from the east coast."

"What about jobs?" someone called out.

"Plenty for everyone. Construction, maintenance, administration, hospitality. I assure you, everyone will prosper. Small businesses, families. Local government." He winked at the mayor. "I hear you need a new sewage treatment plant."

The room hummed as Younger fielded questions. After about twenty minutes he made an announcement.

135

"It's a hot evening, folks. So we're going to wrap it up. Just as soon as we hear from one of the most highly esteemed members of the Cranberry Beach community. We'll be contacting the rest of the property owners in the next week or so. And we've brought you a treat so don't run off after the meeting. Just outside the door is a refrigerated truck full of cold, delicious ice cream. And about fifty kinds of toppings."

A cheer went up.

"But first I want to ask Mick Mahoney to come up here."

Mick's stomach dropped like a rock. Everyone turned around to look at him.

Anna stood beside him at the back wall. She whispered in his ear.

"Don't go up just yet. I've got to say something."

Mick was afraid she was going to embarrass herself. "Anna, why is this so important to you?"

She took a creased and faded piece of paper out of her backpack and pressed it into Mick's hand. Grains of sand stuck to Amanda's drawing of the baby sea turtle.

Anna raised her hand to speak.

Younger looked pained.

"SeaMist seems to be promising a great deal to the people of Cranberry Beach in return for—what?" Anna asked in a surprisingly full and audible voice. She strode to the front of the room. Chairs creaked as people turned to whisper and exchange glances with their neighbors.

Spreading his hands, Younger looked around incredulously. "You're getting jobs, income, a tourism base."

"But what do they have to give SeaMist in return?"

"A little worthless land is all. SeaMist is basically handing prosperity to Cranberry Beach on a silver platter."

Anna gave a signal and Loretta switched on the projector. A photo of a barred security gate appeared on the front wall to the right of the posters.

"Rendezvous Ridge," Anna said. "A SeaMist resort in the Smoky Mountains."

136

Younger raised his hand in a gesture of stopping traffic. "That isn't relevant to this project."

Loretta, hunched over the computer, tapped some keys. Another picture of a big security gate appeared.

"Sunfish Shoals, Florida," Anna announced.

Two more pictures of gates, one with a guard. "Eden East, Texas. Paradise Point, Maui. These are all SeaMist developments and they're all gated. Exclusive. Nobody gets in except guests and residents."

Younger clearly hadn't expected this.

"Will the Cranberry Beach resort be gated?" Anna asked him.

"Probably," Younger admitted. "It's typical for developments like this."

"So if the kids who live here—in the *real* Cranberry Beach—want to swim, they won't be able to go over and swim in your pools."

"Well, uh, I'm sure arrangements can be made . . . uh, for special occasions."

A murmur rippled through the room. He whispered something to his assistant and she slipped out the side door.

Anna continued. "About those jobs. Can you guarantee ongoing employment for the people of the peninsula?"

Younger hesitated half a second. "Of course. Well, theoretically. The applicant's skills have to match our needs."

"What about salary requirements?"

"Uh . . . we're competitive."

A picture appeared on the wall. A newspaper article.

"Here's a report from the New York Times dated about two years ago. It says SeaMist was indicted for illegally importing workers from Central America, paying them shamefully poor wages and quietly shipping them back home if they got sick or injured. Lots cheaper than paying for health care. Some say the accusations amount to human trafficking."

Younger glanced at the side door. The assistant and several teenagers she had drafted were carrying in five-gallon containers of ice cream.

"The indictment was dismissed," he said.

Loretta put another picture on the wall.

"Here's a more recent article about two of SeaMist's corporate officials. They're charged with grand larceny, falsifying business records and violating State of New York business laws."

"I can't comment on that," Younger said. "But legal challenges are a part of any big corporation."

He gestured toward the table set up with frosty tubs of ice cream, toppings, napkins, spoons and bowls.

"If there are more questions, we can talk with people individually. Let's get Mick Mahoney up here for a minute, then we can finish up the evening with an old fashioned ice cream social." He waved Mick up to the front.

Mick's felt like his feet were encased in concrete, as though he were about to be tossed off a pier. He went and stood beside Younger.

Anna called out over the noise of chatting and scooting chairs. "Wait a minute. I have one more question."

"I'm glad to talk with you afterwards, ma'am," Younger said, reaching for Mick's arm.

Mick's guts twisted. He had no idea what he would say.

A new picture appeared on the wall, this time a beach lined with a row of oil derricks. The sand was fouled with black crude oil.

"What is SeaMist doing to preserve wildlife habitat and native species on the island?" Anna asked.

"SeaMist will fulfill the requirements of all shoreline management and environmental protection laws." He smiled patronizingly. "We have to. We won't get our permits unless we do."

Laughter chittered across the room. Shoreline protection laws were a constant irritation on the peninsula.

Anna increased the volume of her voice so that it carried over the twittering. She swept her hand toward the picture.

"This is an island off the gulf coast of Texas. SeaMist bought it with the declared intention of developing a resort. But they found out oil drilling would make more money. Somehow they got around wildlife protection laws. This was a nesting beach for some of the world's most endangered species."

Someone shouted, "Turtles?"

Anna waited until a wave of chuckling died down. "Yes, as a matter of fact."

Another voice called out, "Found any turtles here yet?"

Hoots of laughter and boos erupted.

"You don't even live here," someone shouted. "So you can take your environmental bullshit back to Seattle or Eugene or wherever the hell you come from."

Anna bravely stood her ground. She gestured to the picture of oil derricks. "Do you want that?"

"Oh bull," someone yelled. "We don't have oil on this coast."

"That's just stupid," someone else shouted. "Get out of here, you half-assed hippie."

Someone threw a wadded up ball of paper at her.

Younger called for order. "Let's just hear Mick now and then we can get to our ice cream—which is melting."

The room quieted to a low-frequency grumble.

Anna's cheeks were pink and when she turned to Mick her blue eyes glistened. He discovered, to his surprise, that his confusion was gone.

"I have something to say to all of you," Mick said, "But first I have to say a few words about Anna Davis here. She is a scientist, doing independent research. She's a very smart lady and she knows things most of us have never imagined. And she's probably done us a very big favor tonight. So we need to give her our respect and think seriously about what she's said."

The crowd hushed. Oakley scowled.

Anna smiled at the audience and went back to stand by Loretta.

Gesturing to the picture of the oil derricks, Mick said, "Maybe we don't have oil around here. Maybe we do and nobody knows it. Or nobody's telling. These days it seems like they'll dig for it anywhere. But what we need to get out of Ms. Davis's presentation tonight is that maybe there's a trade-off we're not going to be happy with some day in the future. We need to think about this carefully."

Oakley was coming toward him with a kick-ass look in his eyes.

"Looking at these pictures, I don't think SeaMist knows anything about real community where everybody cares for each other, where everybody's life is connected with everybody else's. But here in Cranberry Beach—the *real* Cranberry Beach—we know about it and have for generations. And I don't want to trade that for easy money and easy promises.

"What I want to say tonight is that I made a stupid kind of a trade-off a long time ago. And now, not only have I lost my family's land, I might have to lose the thing I've always valued most. The respect and goodwill of my neighbors."

He looked around at a hundred familiar faces. Alert, expectant, confused faces. He had grown up with most of them. The community had always been like one big extended family.

Wally Walgren leaned forward to listen, the oxygen line hooked over his ears. He had driven the pickup truck that carried Mick in the parade so many years ago. The thought of disappointing the old man was like a knife in his heart.

Mick took SeaMist's offer of sale out of his pocket and unfolded it.

"I made my last mortgage payment today. I've got no more money, no way of getting any. I'll be in default in a few weeks. So my land is gone. What the storm didn't take, SeaMist will get—one way or another."

He held the sales offer up over his head for everyone to see.

"This is the offer that SeaMist made for my land. But I'm not selling to them."

He tore up the offer and let the pieces fall to the floor.

"There's something else I've got to tell you too. Something I should have been honest about more than forty years ago."

11

Mick leaned gratefully into the work of rowing, with every oar stroke sliding farther away from the scene of his confession. Standing in the bow, Benny stretched his nose toward the island shore, noisily inhaling the night sea aromas. Anna sat on the stern seat, her silver hair shimmering in the starlight.

Tonight he had been stirred by Anna's courage and passion. Seeing her at the meeting valiantly defending what she knew to be right and true, Mick's own sense of rightness had risen up and compelled him to speak his own truth.

The meeting had gone silent in response to his stumbling words. It had felt to him as if he were performing an act of indecent exposure, deliberately revealing the ugliness he had kept hidden so many years. Oakley, charging toward Mick as he tore up the offer of sale, had stopped short, paled, shook his head as if to clear it. He looked to Younger, incredulous, for some sort of explanation. Younger turned away and pulled off his microphone headset in a gesture of disgust, of throwing in the towel.

Mick hadn't said he had been under the threat of blackmail. Only that he had let the lie go on too long, that he regretted it and wanted to be straight with them. The people had listened quietly, with neutral expressions, not whispering to their companions, not muttering sounds of regret or disapproval. It was impossible to know how they were taking it.

He had gone over to Wally afterwards and apologized. The old man had teared up but had said nothing. Irmalene avoided his eyes but patted Mick's hand as she helped Wally turn his walker toward the ice cream table.

Bev forgave him immediately. She squeezed his arm and smiled up at him, her wrinkled old eyes damp behind the thick glasses. She didn't even need time to think about it.

"It doesn't make any difference to me what you did when you were a youngster," she said. "I know you're a good man. And I love you. We all do, you'll see."

Everyone else went directly to the ice cream table after Mick's short speech, casting their eyes away from him, leaving him alone with his shame.

Oakley slunk out the side door with Younger. Later Mick saw them in the parking lot, Younger speaking tersely into his phone, probably to his superiors. He heard Oakley interjecting something that sounded defensive.

Most people departed clutching SeaMist's glossy resort prospectus. To the few who would take them, Loretta and Anna distributed photocopies of their research on SeaMist. As Mick helped them carry their gear back to the library, he caught some questioning, irritated, perhaps disapproving glances from the people he passed.

Now, rowing Anna's boat across the channel through the warm, moonless night, Mick let his troubled thoughts drain away through the oars and sink into the dark water. He could no longer imagine his future. Nor could he remember his past. There was only the present moment, the sensation of his muscles flexing, the breathing in and out of sea-scented air, the exquisite beauty of the starry sky.

And there was something else he couldn't define. He was enlivened in some remarkable way, as if the sparkling phosphorescence he stirred up with his oars flowed from the sea into the waters of his body.

When the keel bumped the beach Benny jumped off and trotted away. Mick waded in ankle-deep water to steady the boat as Anna stepped out. She shouldered her backpack and passed a bag of groceries for him to carry. As he followed close behind her around the curve of the beach to her campsite, he marveled at her ability to see in starlight. Alone, he would have needed a flashlight to keep from tripping over rocks or beach junk, but Anna insisted on a

142

minimum of artificial light which was confusing for turtle hatchlings, a concern that was far-fetched but endearing.

Inside the driftwood enclosure that formed her camp, she kneeled, reached under a driftwood log, and took out a bottle.

"Storm booty," she said, rummaging in the dark for cups.

They sat side by side on tattered lawn chair cushions salvaged from the storm debris with their backs against a log. The gentle surf, far down the beach at low tide, sang softly to itself. Anna poured whiskey into two chipped teacups and handed one to Mick.

"Jack Daniels," she said. "A full bottle, never opened."

She burrowed her bare feet into the warm sand, Benny nestled beside her.

"I'm sorry they weren't too receptive to what you were trying to tell them," Mick said.

"No matter. Our message was bound to be unpopular. But maybe it will sink in. Maybe people will at least consider it."

"Maybe." He reached for the bottle and refilled his cup.

"You know," Anna said, "I wasn't sure you weren't going to sell to SeaMist until you tore up that offer. And the other thing you said in the meeting--I'm curious as to why you chose that particularly *public* time and place."

The humiliation he had felt at the meeting revisited him, crawling warmly up his neck. "My choices were severely limited."

"Ah. I see." She was quiet for a few minutes. "So we can add blackmail to SeaMist's list of criminal activities." Her voice was tight with anger. "That doesn't surprise me. It looks like they might be connected to some high level criminal organizations. But nobody's been able to pin anything on them—yet."

She opened a package of crackers, passed a handful to Mick and gave one to Benny. "It took a lot of courage for you to stand up to them that way." Her voice was softer now, relaxed again.

"I don't look forward to going back to work tomorrow, wondering what my neighbors think of me."

"It's probably not as big a deal as you imagine."

"That I smoked dope and got kicked out of the Navy and lied about it?"

"That was a long time ago. Maybe your neighbors will see you in a little different light now. Maybe you'll have to earn back some of their trust. But I don't think it's serious."

"I should have gone to jail like Sean had to." A paroxysm of grief knotted up his throat and flooded his eyes with tears.

"No, no." She reached over and gently squeezed his hand. "Sean shouldn't have had to go to jail and neither should you. Marijuana is the *least* of the world's problems."

He recalled that his one and only ingestion of weed so many years ago had resulted in nothing more than giggling and a heightened appreciation of potato chips. And strawberry jam.

"Anyway," Anna said, "It's legal now and you don't even have to buy it."

"What?"

She grinned. "A certain variety of *Cannabis sativa* is starting to grow wild all around the Pacific Northwest, in ditches alongside roads and in river valleys and on the edges of marshes. It's an effect of global warming. This species has found climate change quite favorable. But it's not one of the high-powered hybrids they grow under artificial conditions. It's a variety more like the mild stuff we had in the 60s. In a few years there will be enough that people can just go out and pick it—for free. No high priced stores and no black market. And no taxes for the state, though they'll probably try to keep regulating it."

"Where did it come from?"

"Illegal cultivation plots hidden in the woods produced some unexpected, natural hybridization that resulted in a plant that's fairly resilient in our climate conditions. In the past, when it was colder and wetter, it was hard for the seeds to germinate and grow to maturity without help from human gardeners. Now it's easy. The seeds are scattered by birds and animals. They're sprouting up everywhere."

"You've seen it around here?"

"I'll show you a place right on this little island."

They were quiet for a few minutes while Mick tried to take in that information.

144

"Want to try some?" Anna started to get up. "It's probably dry by now."

Mick shook his head, scandalized and curious at the same time. He had not been one of the voters who had made it legal to buy and use marijuana in the State of Washington. But after it was legalized he had been tempted once or twice to go incognito into Longview and buy some to try. There was no way to get around the guilt though.

"I understand," Anna said, sitting down again. "Too soon. You can think about it."

Mick thought that Anna was pretty much the most interesting person he had ever encountered.

"I don't usually like to smoke it," she said.

"Brownies then?"

"You should try my triple chocolate herbal torte. It's only for very special occasions."

Mick tossed back his whiskey and reached for the bottle again. Anna held out her cup for a refill.

"This is my substance of choice right now," he said, "But maybe later . . ." He wanted to leave the door open.

After a few minutes she asked, "When's your birthday?"

"January."

He tried to think about January and got nowhere.

"Will I still know you in January?" he asked.

"Why not?"

"You'll have to go back to work, to Newport."

"It isn't so far away."

"And I might have to leave Cranberry Beach. Don't know where I'll be in January."

"But this is your home."

"Not any more. My land is gone--really, literally gone. Or will be in a few weeks, after the foreclosure. And the folks here aren't going to want me around after what I told them tonight."

"Mick." She shifted to look at him. "You did something incredibly important tonight. You set your soul back in balance.

Whenever someone does that it restores a little bit of balance to the world's soul. People feel that. They're blessed by it."

A few weeks ago he would have dismissed these words as new age bullshit. But tonight he let them ease his anxiety a bit.

Anna took his hand again and held it firmly. "It wouldn't be right for you to have to leave this beautiful place," she said. "Even if you don't own it in a legal sense, it still belongs to you in all the important ways. And you love it with all your heart."

That was true.

She released his hand and leaned back to look at the sky. "What a pleasure it is to live on the earth," she sighed. "All those stars," she saluted them with her cup, "lighting up the night like this."

Mick had lived here all his life but he had never seen a night quite like this before, with the Milky Way a shimmering banner so bright the ocean reflected its light.

Anna stood up. "Let's walk."

Benny ran ahead of them, sniffing thoughtfully at every mound of seaweed he encountered. Mick and Anna waded knee deep into the swirling water, a pleasant coolness contrasting with the warm air, nothing like the muscle-cramping cold it had always been until recently.

"Wait a minute." Mick peered around in the dusky water. "What about those jellyfish?"

Anna laughed. "There's been an offshore wind. They've all blown away for a while."

They walked in the water along the beach as it curved around into the channel then moved up onto the damp, packed sand and sat down. The surf quieted to a ripple there, sliding obliquely across the sand. A few lights twinkled across the water at Cranberry Beach.

"Look at that sky, down near the horizon," she said, sweeping her hand toward the far edge of the sea. "The color of blue velvet. Or the ink that used to be in blue fountain pens."

She turned to follow the horizon around to the north, looking behind them at the India ink silhouettes of pine trees against the dark blue sky.

146

"Well, Holy Mother of God!" She stood up and pointed to the sky. "Will you look at that!"

Mick got up and turned around.

Northern lights danced in the sky above the tree tops. Blue and green curtains of celestial light fluttered in the solar wind with stars peeping through the gauzy veils.

"Oh my God," Mick whispered. He had never, ever, seen the aurora before. It had been reported locally many times in the last few months, an effect of a cyclic peak of sunspot activity. But he had never been awake or outside when it was happening. He remembered scientists explaining on TV that the display of colors was a side effect of the earth protecting itself from the hot, harmful intrusions of gaseous sun belches. But nothing had prepared him for the beauty of it. It was like an arrow in his heart.

"Heaven," was the only word he could think of.

Anna glanced at his face then turned back to the gorgeous sight.

"Heavenly, yes," she said.

"I mean . . ." Mick shook his head, groping for words. "The place where Sean is . . . heaven. I mean . . . I don't believe in it. But with Sean gone sometimes I wish I believed in religion or God or something."

"Maybe it would bring some kind of meaning to his death and to your suffering."

He felt the sting of grief in his throat. It would be comforting to think that Sean was up there floating around in those glowing, celestial clouds, benevolently looking down on his Dad. But religion bringing meaning to suffering? That was a stretch.

"Do you believe in God, Anna?"

"I call it the Great Mystery. But God is another word for the feeling."

"You said in the storm that you don't have a formal religion. What *do* you believe in?"

She held her arms up over her head as if to gather the whole sky to her heart, then pointed to a shore pine outlined in black against the peacock blue aurora.

"There's what I believe in—the Tree of Life."

"So . . . is that a religion?" If it was, Mick had never heard of it.

"No, I don't think so. It's a story. Or a picture or diagram kind of thing. Or a blueprint. If you want to tell the story of the universe, how it began and evolved and how the earth came to be and how all of us—bacteria and jellyfish, buttercups and humans-- got to be here, you can trace it out as if it were a tree."

Anna was moving like a dancer now, arms swaying to the sky, hands forming pictures.

"Its taproot reaches back to the very beginning of the universe. The Big Bang. And everything unfolds from there. The first stars come into being and the stars explode and their dust makes new stars and so on and so on and so on."

Her arms and hands made exploding stars and whirling galaxies.

"And then our grandmother star is born and dies and her dust makes the sun and the planets and our mother Gaia Earth."

She traced on the sky a stem that branched into three big trunks, then sketched little branches coming off the main ones.

"And things get more and more complex and diverse and that's like the branches of the tree. Every kind of living thing that's made of stardust has its place on a branch of the tree. And the branches are growing all the time. New kinds of beings evolve, others die off. But the whole thing keeps going."

Mick watched her create beings with her fingers, chanting their names, many in the strangely poetic cadence of scientific Latin. She placed them on branches like ornaments on a Christmas tree.

"Spirochetes . . . thermoproteus . . . flagellates . . . fungi . . . gymnosperms . . . arachnids . . . squid . . . snails . . . reptiles . . . sea turtles . . ."

He sat down, dizzy from looking up too much. Anna's picture glowed in the back of his brain like the after-image from looking at something too bright.

After what seemed like a long list of names, she paused, brought her hands together in a gesture of prayer, stood quietly for a while, then sat down beside him on the sand.

"So many beings, it's impossible to name them all," she said. "And we only know the earth ones."

Something tickled his right foot. He brushed at it absently, wondering what Anna meant by the "earth ones."

Benny pressed his nose to Mick's hand, sniffing. He felt another tickle, this time on his left calf and thought it must be Benny, but the dog was still on his right. Benny made a growly, warbling sound in his throat and cocked his head, looking at whatever was crawling along beside Mick's leg.

"What's up Benny?" Anna said as she gazed at the sky.

Benny went around to her, repeated his growly yodel and pawed at her arm.

Mick felt something little tapping along his foot.

It was hard to see in the dark but slowly the scene came into focus. At first it seemed the sand around them flowed like a brook over stones. Then he saw that it was a river of tiny sand-colored creatures moving toward the sea.

"Anna . . ."

She looked down.

"Oh my God. It's them." She gazed at Mick, wide-eyed. "Or am I dreaming again?"

"I don't think so. If you're dreaming, then I am too."

She picked up one of the creatures and examined it. "Turtles. Oh, my God, it's baby turtles." When she released it the baby turtle clambered straight on toward the sea.

"Don't get up," she said. "There's a chance we might step on them. They're vulnerable when they're on the beach, hard to see and easy pickings for all sorts of predators."

She twisted to look behind her toward the upper beach. "I wonder where the nest is. How could I have missed the tracks?"

"What tracks?"

149

"About a month ago there would have been what look like parallel tractor tire tracks in the sand where the mother drags herself up the beach with her flippers. That's how you can find the nests, just follow those tracks. But wind can erase them pretty quickly."

"How many are there?"

"Depending on the species there can be anywhere from 30 to 100 eggs to a nest, though not all of them hatch."

Benny trotted up the beach in the direction Anna was looking, following the trail of tiny, scrabbling creatures. A few minutes later he barked sharply. A hissing growl answered. Then a volley of fierce barking from Benny.

"Sounds like Benny found a raccoon plundering the nest."

When it seemed the parade of turtles had ended, she stood up. "I think we can move now, but be careful. There might be a few stragglers."

She stepped carefully up the beach. Not wanting to feel a wriggling crunch under his bare feet, Mick followed Anna closely, trying to place his feet where she did.

Benny led them to the nest, a dim ragged hole in the sand. A few unhatched ping-pong ball shaped eggs remained. Two tiny dead bodies lay nearby. Their chewed up appearance suggested they were victims of the raccoon.

Benny growled, glancing at Anna as he stalked toward a clump of brush.

"Is it in there? Good boy, Benny." Anna picked up a piece of driftwood and flung it hard at the brush. A hissing growl and rustling of leaves accompanied the raccoon's departure.

"The rule in dealing with endangered species is never to interfere with natural processes," she said. "But I've got to convince some people to move fast to protect these little guys. So I'm going to collect these two dead ones and some eggs. In the past I've had a license to collect but when I left my job in North Carolina I couldn't get it renewed. Doing this could get me in big trouble, depending on how National Marine Fisheries looks at it, whether they think I killed them or they died in my care. So you're my witness. But it should be pretty clear they died from raccoon bites."

150

"You know, Mick said, "There was one guy, a few years back, who picked up an adult sea turtle that had washed up on the beach south of here. He was convicted of killing it. They found the shell in his garage. He spent some time in jail and got a big fine."

"That was what—about fifteen years ago?"

"Yeah. Something like that."

"Back then federal agencies had barely enough funding to support prosecutions. Now they're struggling to survive. That's why I've got to get to Seattle first thing in the morning, evidence in hand. Before anyone else finds out what we've got here. I have to convince the Office for Law Enforcement to put some immediate protections on this island. A court order. And SeaMist isn't going to like it."

"So this could block the resort?"

"It's possible. But SeaMist can get around restraining orders—legally or otherwise—if they move fast enough."

"Shit."

"Right. So what I need you to do is stay right here and guard this nest with Benny. If the raccoon comes back chase it away. I'll be right back."

Waiting for Anna to return with her camera and notebook, Mick looked up at a night sky that seemed to be filled with new stars and uncharted constellations. If someone had told him a few weeks ago that tonight he would be guarding a turtle nest, he would have laughed at the joke. Now he had to give up on even trying to imagine what was going to come next.

12

Dawn tinted the sky over the eastern hills when Mick, with Anna and Benny beside him, swung his pickup into the parking lot of the Cranberry Beach library. A few minutes later Loretta's ancient blue VW bug slid to a stop next to them.

She squeezed herself out from behind the steering wheel and tugged at the seat of her shorts before hobbling to the library door in what appeared to be bedroom slippers.

"Thank you so much!" Anna said as she followed Loretta in. "I'm so sorry to get you up this early."

Loretta waved away the apology. "No problem. Glad to help."

She went around flipping on lights and powering up the two computers. Bending to pet Benny, she said, "What a good dog you are. You made a big discovery, didn't you. A turtle dog you are."

Benny wagged and licked her face then rolled on his back and pedaled his legs gleefully.

Loretta sat down at the computer next to Anna and got busy on the keyboard. "I'm sending you the list I put together after you called. It's most of the organizations you asked for. I'll get the Sierra Club and state Fish and Wildlife in a minute."

"Good—excellent. I've got it. Thank you again," Anna said, tapping away at her own computer. "I'm downloading the pictures from last night. Here, take a look."

Loretta rolled her chair over and looked at Anna's screen. "Well, for heaven's sake, would you look at that. Incredible!"

Mick marveled at the technical abilities of the two women. The computer age had passed him by. Sometimes he felt like the last human on earth without email.

Loretta waved him toward the coffeemaker. Now that was something he was good at. As the fragrance of coffee filled the room he hovered behind the two women. Photos of the nest and the dead baby turtles appeared on the email messages Anna typed on her screen.

"Okay, I'm sending to your phone a list of the Seattle addresses you want to visit," Loretta said. "I'll start making phone calls to the people you've emailed as soon as their offices open this morning. Then I'll relay any responses to your phone."

Anna nodded. "Good. Could you brief Sheriff Grayson about what we've discovered? And keep it low key, but remind him about the Endangered Species Act. He won't like it, but tell him I'm going to do my best to get the feds involved. Try to convince him of how important it is to keep the discovery out of the public eye for a few days."

Loretta nodded as she typed. "I'll do that. And I'll keep digging on SeaMist too."

Anna stopped what she was doing to reach over and give Loretta a brief hug. "You're amazing Loretta."

Loretta chuckled. "I know. Do you want Benny to stay with me while you're gone?"

Anna stopped turned to Benny. "What do you think, Benny? Do you want to stay with Loretta?"

The dog wagged and gave a short woof then licked Loretta's bare knee.

The women laughed. "Okay then," Anna said.

* * *

Mick drove toward Seattle listening as Anna talked on the phone with Maury. She had already called him in the middle of the night after discovering the turtles, but now there was more scientific-sounding information to share.

153

She hung up and checked her voice mail messages.

"Hah—Loretta's good. She's already talked with somebody from the Sierra Club. He's going to call her back in an hour or so."

Mick checked his watch. A little after seven. "Someone's in their office this early in the morning?"

"A lot of people in Seattle work on east coast time."

She tried keying in a number. "Damn. Now there's no service."

"No cell towers in these hills. It should be back by the time we get to Elma," Mick said. "Are you tired? Do you want to take a nap?"

"Hell, no. I'm too excited to sleep."

"Okay. Tell me about your government job."

"I'm a research fisheries biologist with the Fishery Resource Analysis and Monitoring Division of the National Marine Fisheries."

"Right." Mick laughed. "And you do what?"

"A boring job mostly involving digging away at a database in a basement office at the Newport Research Station. I collect data on groundfish."

"Not turtles?"

"Not officially. But I took the job because it puts me in contact with lots of fishery observers who work in the North Pacific. And they talk to lots of people who work on fishing boats. I've been getting information on turtle sightings at sea that way for several years. Doing my own research on the side."

"Why don't you have a job studying turtles?"

"I worked with sea turtles in North Carolina until about six years ago. But after the dream, the one I told you about during the storm, I wanted to study them here on the Pacific Northwest coast. That idea didn't fly with my supervisors."

"Wait a minute. You didn't live on the west coast when you had that dream of Cranberry Beach?"

"No. I hadn't even been here before."

"And you clearly saw the Cranberry Beach water tower in your dream?"

"Yes."

154

"But how could you have known what it would look like?"

She paused before answering. "I think dreams—some dreams anyway—come from other than our own memories or imaginations."

This seemed way off the deep end of logic.

"Wait. Hold on there. You transferred to a boring job on the west coast only because of that dream?"

She considered for a few minutes. "Basically, yes. But the dream only pointed to a direction for inquiry. Other facts supported the idea that the sea turtles might be moving north. Increased numbers of strandings on Northwest beaches for one thing. Reports of turtles actively swimming north of fifty degrees latitude for another. And one other unexplained phenomenon.

"The Seattle Aquarium has been the Northwest Center for Sea Turtle Rehabilitation for many years. Turtles washed up on northwest beaches are taken there for treatment of hypothermia and whatever other illnesses they come in with. When they're nursed back to health they're flown down to California, fitted with satellite transmitters, and released in San Diego Bay. And nearly every one tracked in the last ten years has headed straight north again and continued in that direction until their transmitters quit. Two have even returned to the same beaches where they were originally found."

"Let me guess. Cranberry Beach."

"That was one of them. Grayland was the other."

"Jeez. Why do you think they're doing that?"

"Nobody knows. The truth is, sea turtle behavior is not well understood. You would think, since they're so acutely endangered, that they would be studied more. But most of the federal research money goes to fisheries, to study food fish. A politically expedient approach to allocation of scarce funds."

"You said before that you've written papers. Why were they rejected?"

"I couldn't get a grant to go out and actually count sea turtles. All I had was anecdotal information, stories from fishermen. Which is a second class kind of data in the scientific world. And I had no support from my supervisors in North Carolina. In fact, they told me that if I continued with my research on north Pacific turtles I would be fired. Nobody wanted any public relations fiascos."

"What do you mean? What were they afraid of?"

"It was hard enough to get shrimp fishermen in the Gulf of Mexico to use turtle excluder devices on their nets to keep from accidentally catching and killing them. What kind of uproar do you think fishermen in the northwest would make if they're told they can't fish unless they change their gear? How would people in coastal communities respond if told they can't use the beaches the way they want to because turtles could be nesting on them?"

They rode in silence for a while, through thousands of acres of formerly wooded landscape charred by a recent forest fire. The thick underbrush typical of forests west of the Cascade Mountains had been tinder dry for years now and ignited with the smallest spark. The northwest had been hit by droughts several times in Mick's lifetime and always recovered. But this year was different. The intense rain generated by the summer's one superstorm had gouged deep gullies down every denuded hillside but had done little to green anything up. And there hadn't been any more rain to speak of in the several weeks since Sean had died.

"So you think it's global warming that brought the turtles to our beach?" he asked.

"Warming of the sea and the sand has created favorable habitat for them here, at least for now. That's quite clear. But choosing a new nesting beach is unprecedented. It's never been observed anyway. When I was a graduate student, I was involved in a project in Texas to relocate turtle nests to a safer spot after what had been a federally protected beach was opened up for gas drilling. We dug up eggs and re-nested them on a different beach, then tagged the hatchlings before they went into the sea. Twenty years later when they were sexually mature, most of those hatchlings that survived to adulthood returned to the original beach to nest, not to the safer beach where they had hatched.

156

"That's just one of a thousand mysteries about sea turtles. But the important thing about them for us humans, at this point in our history, is that the turtles and all the other endangered species are canaries in our coal mine. And global warming is one of the dangers their early demise is warning us about."

"One of the dangers. What else is hanging over our heads?"

"The world is in a huge mess. Terrorism, pollution, violence and injustice of every kind, starvation. Everybody has something to add to that list. Essentially, we all feel it, if we aren't shutting it out. The world isn't right. Things are out of kilter. And I think it comes down to a very basic problem. We're out of balance with the natural world because we've used technology to set ourselves outside the laws of natural selection. We've sidestepped many of the natural regulating mechanisms of population growth. And now there are too many of us to support with available technology. There are too few resources and those resources are not shared equitably. Not among human populations and not with most other life forms either."

"So how does global warming fit into that?" Mick asked.

"It's a big effect of unbalanced natural processes. And it's clearly human activity that has tipped the scales."

"But some people say this is just part of a natural variation in climate. Not all the scientists are preaching doom and gloom."

"A few always go against the commonly accepted theories. That's part of the healthy skepticism of the scientific process. And it's really only a handful of scientists. The media tends to exaggerate to sell news. But when you look at what the opposition is saying, it's mostly a matter of quibbling over details. And, of course, a few of the dissenters are on the payrolls of government or corporate entities interested in maintaining the status quo.

"But the anthropogenic signal is fully confirmed by essentially all the world's climate experts. There's no question that abruptly rising carbon dioxide levels correlate on exactly the same staggeringly steep curve as rising temperatures. And that corresponds precisely with the beginning and advancement of the industrial revolution . . . ."

157

Mick's attention faltered. The scientific stuff was bouncing off his head. He tried to hold up his end of the conversation.

"So if we just go back to living like cavemen, then the natural world would be right again?" he asked.

"No. Even if we stop all release of greenhouse gases immediately, the warming process is long-term. There's no shutting it off. Maybe the effects can be lessened. But for the most part the damage has been done. We're just going to have to adapt to the consequences somehow."

A mile out of Elma her phone rang. She took notes as she talked, going over the story of how the hatchlings were found. Then she answered a few questions. Her voice was cool and business-like but she tapped her pencil rapidly on the notebook as she spoke.

"Okay," she said when she hung up. "We have an appointment at the the National Marine Fisheries Office of Law Enforcement at 10:30. Think we can make it there by then?"

Mick checked his watch. It was 7:45. In a few minutes they would merge onto Interstate 5 at Olympia where commuter traffic would be leapfrogging for exit positions. From there it would be another sixty-five miles of heavy traffic to Seattle.

"Almost three hours to get there? Maybe. I haven't driven to Seattle in several years."

"It's gotten a lot worse."

It had. They averaged fifteen miles per hour through the Olympia area, speeded up to fifty through the Nisqually delta, then it was red taillights and a snail's crawl through the military bases and Tacoma, which was just as well since the road surface was in serious need of repair.

Anna talked nonstop on her phone now, writing constantly in her notebook. By the time they reached the traffic horrors of Southcenter, she had made three more appointments for later in the afternoon.

Mick maneuvered the truck across three lanes of traffic, exited I-5 and merged to the on-ramp of I-405 only to pull up short behind what looked like a parking lot.

Anna groaned. "It would probably be faster to walk."

"It's only 9:30. We'll get there. And anyway, what's the problem if we're late? Can't you call them?"

"I think OLE is interested enough in what I'm bringing them. They'll probably wait if they need to. But I'm a little afraid they'll detain me and that could make me late for my two o'clock appointment at Pacific Coastal Conservancy, which is downtown."

"Detain you? Like arrest? For not having a collecting permit?"

"It just depends on who we talk to, how literally they follow the rules."

"Just what are you even going there for? It's almost like you're turning yourself in."

"I'm going to ask them to protect that beach, to actually patrol it. Which is not something they're even going to listen to unless I show them this evidence."

She patted the small cooler on the floor by her feet.

"Could they put you in jail?"

"Nah. There's no reason to do that. They'll cite me and I'll have to show up in court sometime later. What they could do is question me for a long time or make us wait. And they'll ask you questions too. They'll want to get the story straight."

Riding the brake pedal as he waited for an opening to slip into a faster-moving lane, Mick considered the strange turn his life had taken. He could have just loaned Anna the truck and gone back to work at the Mercantile. But without even a moment's hesitation he had agreed to drive her through madhouse traffic to an interrogation by federal agents. And now it turned out that his own part in the illegal removal and death of a federally protected species would also be investigated. But what the hell—he didn't have a lot to lose right now and his life in recent weeks, though wrenching, was getting interesting. He owed a lot to Anna Davis. The least he could do was drive her around and possibly go to jail on federal charges.

*   *   *

They arrived at the huge National Oceanic and Atmospheric Administration complex forty minutes late. Special Agent Tom Shepard, a quiet, reserved man in his late forties, met them at the security desk on the first floor. A badge was pinned to his belt but he didn't wear a uniform and Mick could see no other insignia that marked him as a law enforcement officer except for the firearm holstered on his hip.

Shepard was interested. After an initial disclosure of the contents of the cooler he took Anna's paperwork to an assistant to begin verifying her credentials. The cooler he sent away to a lab in an adjoining building. And he separated Mick and Anna.

Three hours later Anna had missed her two o'clock appointment. Mick didn't know where she was or how long he would have to wait for her. Shepard had dismissed him after half an hour of questioning in someone's unoccupied office. Mick had waited in the reception area until hunger and boredom sent him to the building café for a sandwich and coffee.

Now, sitting in the shade of an umbrella on a patio between two glass and steel buildings, he looked across Lake Washington through thick brownish haze, blinking from the acrid air. Seattle sweltered in grimy heat. Traffic clogged every arterial and housing packed every square foot of the neighborhoods they had traveled through. He wondered how anyone could bear to live in the city.

It looked like a lot of the plants had given up. When they drove along highway 520 where it passed through the arboretum, Anna had pointed out trees decimated by viral diseases. Weakened by long-term drought, they hadn't been able to resist what once would have been minor infections. And what had been a green oasis of marsh along the edge of the lake had given way to infestations of smelly algae.

The groundskeepers for the NOAA complex had clearly given up on anything green too. The natural prairie grasses that surrounded the buildings lay flat and brown, unadorned by any kind of leafy shrubs or flowered plantings.

160

Maybe it *was* global warming. Anna had sketched a jagged pattern in the air with her finger as Mick drove the jostling freeways. Many ups and downs of more or less equal height represented the natural fluctuations in climate over thousands, even millions of years. And then she had swooped her finger nearly straight up to the right, off the scale. The industrial revolution and the burning of coal, then oil, gasoline and a host of other petrochemical products had produced what scientists called the anthropogenic signal, meaning man-made. And it was different from anything ever before in the ancient or recent histories of climate.

At home in Cranberry Beach, it was easy for Mick to shrug the idea away. Air always smelled good there, though Anna said it was tainted with pollution from Chinese coal-fired power plants. But here in Seattle the pollution was always in your face and eyes and you could taste it. You could see dirt everywhere. Tiny particles of soot rained down on every surface. And that wasn't even the most dangerous stuff. She had told him it was the invisible carbon dioxide belching from every tailpipe that was the big problem. And even though gas prices had gone through the roof in the last decade, few people drove their cars less or used public transportation more, or rode bikes or walked or drove high fuel efficiency or electric vehicles.

Most people in Cranberry Beach felt it necessary for each person in their family over sixteen to have their own car and drive it at will. For getting to work and doing errands and taking vacations. For convenience. For independence. It was probably the same for people in Seattle. Hell, Mick thought. It's the way we do things. He couldn't see any way to change it.

Anna joined him, looking tired but pleased.

"How'd it go?" he asked.

"I think we'll get some action. How soon and how much I don't know. They want to send someone out to look at the site."

"Was it tough—the interrogation?" Mick teased a little. "They slap you around any?"

She laughed. "I didn't crack."

"They confiscate the turtles?"

"Of course. Shepard showed them around to some of the biologists here. Nobody could identify the species, which is actually hard to do when they're little. They wasted a lot of time on that. Then they wasted a lot more time trying to find out who I was, even though I am an *employee* of the National Marine Fisheries. They had to call my old supervisors in North Carolina and that took a long time. Then they farted around getting copies of my old collecting permit applications faxed up here."

"So they decided you were okay then? Are they going to prosecute you?"

"I don't know at this point. They'll take their time. It's all new so they have to go slow, investigate it all. But I worry that they'll go too slow and something bad will happen to any other nests that might be on the beach. SeaMist probably wouldn't hesitate to destroy them if they think it will keep their project on track."

"Hey, do you want something to eat?" Mick pointed to the sandwiches and espresso machine behind the counter. "An iced latte?"

"Sounds good." They got up and headed toward the café.

"Is there any way to get these people to move faster?" he asked.

"Only if someone actually breaks the law in a more definite way than I did. Shepard and his supervisors didn't like my having the dead babies and eggs but after a while they accepted my story and the fact that I had applied for a collecting permit. They still don't think I'm enough of an expert on sea turtles though. They want to get someone up here from North Carolina or Texas who currently works with turtles. But it's not clear yet whether travel funds are available. And they won't be completely convinced that an endangered species has decided to nest on our beach until their own expert tells them it's so."

The barista slid Anna's iced drink across the counter.

"So there's nothing we can do but wait for them to figure it all out?"

"No—there's a lot we can do. Ready to drive in downtown Seattle traffic?"

162

She grinned, poked a straw through the plastic lid of her drink, shouldered her backpack and led the way out of the building.

* * *

At seven o'clock that evening they ordered drinks before dinner on the vine-covered patio of a Thai restaurant in Old Ballard. It was a welcome respite after an exhausting afternoon of meetings. But the day's work wasn't over yet. One more meeting was scheduled for later that evening there in the restaurant.

Anna had checked them into rooms two blocks away at the Moon Garden Bed and Breakfast, insisting it wouldn't be safe to drive all the way back to Cranberry Beach when neither of them had had any sleep for more than thirty-six hours.

A beautiful young woman brought a green tinted cocktail in a frosty glass and set it down in front of Anna.

"I didn't figure you for a martini person," Mick said.

She lifted the delicate stemmed glass and sipped some of the shimmering liquid.

"I don't always swig straight out of the bottle," she said, grinning. "And this isn't a classic martini. It's one of Madam Ming's patented concoctions. She adds herbal tinctures and fruit extracts to a very good vodka."

A hippie drink. He took a long, grateful draw of his Hale's pale ale.

He was completely out of his element in this urban setting. But Anna, amazing woman, seemed quite at home navigating them through traffic, finding parking and getting them to meetings in offices in downtown buildings so high it had made him dizzy to look out the windows.

She had urged him to sit in on the meetings, which were mostly about a lot of legal stuff he didn't understand. Injunctions and restraining orders and amicus briefs. He had no idea how Anna knew about all that, but she sounded competent. She asked a lot of questions, told her story over and over, and got people to agree to things.

Between meetings she had talked on the phone with Loretta, sharing information and getting advice. She talked with people in North Carolina too, and someone in Maryland. And late in the afternoon she had called Tom Shepard to see how the investigation was going.

"How do you know all that stuff?" Mick asked. "About the conservation people and the law?"

"From my old job of course. But I used to volunteer in a conservancy program a number of years ago, when the sea turtles were just beginning to be protected. I worked with some small beach communities in North Carolina."

"And how do you know Loretta?"

"I've used the library computers for email ever since I started spending summers at Cranberry Beach. We got to know each other. She's smart."

"I've known her since high school."

"Did you know she's a private investigator?"

Mick nearly dropped his beer. "What?" He laughed out loud, then quickly wished he had been kinder. Loretta's unkempt gray hair and pudgy body and her bookish ways were far from the sleek, dangerous image he conjured up of a private eye. But maybe she was more like one of those English older lady-detectives featured in British murder mysteries. He laughed again.

Anna cocked an eyebrow.

Mick tried to back up. "I've never noticed that she leaves Cranberry Beach. She must not get many cases."

"She does all her investigations at home or from the library, on the web and phone. The library can't pay her a salary but she works there in return for time on the computer when the library isn't busy, which it seldom is. She could do all her work on her home computer but she thinks Cranberry Beach should have a library so she does what she can to keep it open."

"So she actually makes her living doing investigations?"

"Yes. I gather it's a pretty good living. And she really loves the work."

164

He felt the corners of his lips pulling into a grin. "Does she carry a weapon?"

"Oh, for God's sake." Anna laughed. "She doesn't skulk around or do stake-outs if that's what you mean. She just collects information on people or subjects. Like when investors want to research a company or employers want to check out applicants. And she does some genealogy work too."

He thought he might have gone his whole life without ever knowing that about Loretta.

The waiter brought their appetizer, a round tray of tiny dishes mounded with various condiments and encircled with dark green, heart-shaped leaves.

Anna was delighted with the dish. "Have you ever tried this?"

"What is it?"

She said the Thai name which made no impression on him and demonstrated the technique for eating it, rolling the leaf like a burrito around a few roasted peanuts, some coconut, ginger and hot chilies with a dribble of sweet sauce and a paper thin slice of lime. She made one and handed it to Mick.

"Just put the whole thing in your mouth and eat it."

He had never tasted anything like it. A hundred pungent sensations at once, flavors, textures and aromas all in motion, shifting like a kaleidoscope.

The waiter brought another beer for Mick and one for Anna.

"You can't get anything like this in Cranberry Beach," he said, arranging a row of three peanuts on a leaf.

"What do you think? Do you like it?"

"Yeah."

He looked around the patio which was decorated with aged, odd cabinetry, carved wooden deer masks and candle holders dripping with wax.

"How do you know about this place?"

"Maury brought me here once a couple years ago. He grew up in Ballard. His mother still lives here.

Mick rolled condiments into another leaf.

"Actually, it's through Maury's mother that I know Kazuhiro Haglund who's going to meet us here after dinner."

"The banker?"

"The conservation bank specialist. He helps set them up."

Conservation banks. One more technical term to add to the mountain of new things he had learned about today. He could never absorb it all. And it was impossible to see what difference it would make to Cranberry Beach. Maybe the turtles could be saved by all their efforts. But he would still be burdened by his own personal problems.

Gloomy thoughts elbowed their way into his awareness, pushing aside the pleasure of eating. Tomorrow he would return to Cranberry Beach, to face not only foreclosure on his mortgage but also disapproval and rejection by his friends and neighbors. Even though last night Anna had tried to reassure him, he felt certain he would have to start making plans to move away. But where?

"You know," Anna said. "Kaz might really be able to help us. All of us."

"The turtles, you mean."

"The turtles and the humans and all the other species that live on the peninsula. And you in particular."

Mick had meant to ask her to remind him just what a conservation bank was and how it could help him, but their main dishes arrived, requiring complete attention. He recognized some of the ingredients. Prawns, chicken, a scatter of chopped peanuts and green onions over sweetly sauced noodles. But others needed explanation from Anna. Tofu. Lemon grass. A warning about the heat of Thai peppers a few seconds too late. Lacy patterned lotus root. Exotic mushrooms.

She tried to give him a lesson in chopsticks but, frustrated, he tossed them aside in favor of a fork. Too much novelty for one day. Anna promised to show him how to use them some day when he wasn't so hungry. Anna ordered mango ice cream for them and Mick discovered it was another lovely thing he had missed all his life so far.

166

Before the ice cream was gone Kazuhiro Haglund stood before them, smiling broadly. He embraced Anna and offered his hand to Mick.

The waiter brought another bowl of ice cream and Kaz dug into it. He looked more like a playboy than a business man. He was tall, six-four or more, muscular, lanky with light brown skin, faintly almond shaped eyes and black, cropped hair. He wore a red Hawaiian shirt with a cell phone sticking out of the pocket, surfer shorts and flip flops. He couldn't have been more than twenty-five.

"Sorry I couldn't meet with you earlier," he said to Anna. "Just got off a plane. I was in Maui when you called this morning."

"We're lucky you were coming back today," she said.

"Actually, I was supposed to come back next week, but your situation is very interesting. I think we need to jump on it. There's some buzz already." He scraped the bottom of his bowl then dropped the spoon in it and slid it away.

"Who's talking about it?"

"Conservation people. Sierra Club. Some local groups. Word's spreading."

"Oh, dear. I hope there's not going to be any public exposure at this point."

The phone in Kaz's pocket rang. He reached in and turned it off without answering it. "The news media will get ahold of it sometime soon. Timing's going to be real important. What's OLE doing at this point?"

"Not much. They want to look first."

"Okay. Official scientific confirmation. What's happening with that?"

"They want to get an expert in from North Carolina, hopefully in the next couple days."

Kaz grinned. "I talked to Maury today. I'm convinced you're enough of an expert for me. And Loretta Primrose sent me your C.V. along with pictures of the nest and info about the island and everything, including SeaMist."

He nodded to Mick. "Sorry about how you lost your land. We may be able to offer you a fair price for it, if everything comes together the way I think it will. It's going to be a few days before things line up. We'll need to get our financial backers onboard. I know one who is hot to invest in this, but it's a risk because we'll have to move before the feds and the state have time to get this habitat on their official endangered species lists. If that doesn't happen, all we end up with is some real estate."

He turned to Anna. "What this hinges on is whether turtles are going to be showing up on other beaches along the west coast. If we can be reasonably sure this is more than a one-time, one-place phenomenon, it makes a lot of sense to go with a mitigation bank at Cranberry Beach. The only thing is, we don't have time to wait for a survey of other beaches. So it's hunch time. What do you think?"

Anna thought about it. "If it's global warming that's allowing them to migrate north, then I do think others will follow. And there's nothing unique about Cranberry Beach. I wouldn't be surprised to see them in sandy, sheltered bays all along the coast."

Kaz nodded, took the phone out of his pocket and slid out of the booth. "Okay. We'll be in touch." He shook hands again, smiled, and thumbed a number into the phone as he walked away.

"What the hell was he talking about?" Mick asked.

Anna laughed and motioned to the waiter. "Let's get our check. I'll try to explain it as we walk."

The check had already been paid by Kaz.

"Who *is* he?" Mick asked as they walked in the warm evening air.

"A business man. Japanese mother, Norwegian father. Graduated from Antioch University here in Seattle with one of those whole system design degrees combining environmental studies and business. He's set up a number of these conservation banks and made good money at it."

"Wait. He said *mitigation* bank."

"Same thing. What a conservation bank does is mitigate--in a way make up for--environmental damage elsewhere. It's not a perfect answer to habitat destruction problems, not for the endangered species and not for the developers. But it's a way to

168

partially alleviate damage and let at least some development proceed at the same time."

"So the island would be the conservation bank?"

"Yes. Kaz will try to round up one or more investors who can put money into the project. With that money the bank can buy the land on the island. And they'll make it a permanent preserve for marine turtle nests. Then, when a developer wants to build somewhere near other turtle nesting beaches, he can buy credits from the conservation bank to make up for the habitat he's going to impact. That's an oversimplification though. It's quite a bit more complicated than that."

"And the investors end up with more money than they put in?"

"That's the gamble, yes. And so far they've gotten a fair return on their money."

"They'll buy my land? The underwater part too?"

"Yes. If it works out."

The Moon Garden Bed and Breakfast occupied the top floor and roof of an aged but refurbished red brick building in the old part of Ballard. Mick unlatched the wrought iron entry gate and pushed it open as Anna's phone rang, muffled in the pocket of her backpack.

"Oh damn, I've got to get that," she said.

It was Maury, doing something in Newport in support of the turtle protection project. Then her phone beeped a text.

"It's from Loretta," she said frowning. "I'll be up in a minute. I need to borrow the computer in the office to print something off my email."

Mick climbed the stairs to the rooftop suite, unlocked the door, left it open for Anna, and sat on the couch in the shared sitting room between the two bedrooms. The hotel was owned by Jeannie and Paul, two young friends of Anna's who were delighted to provide the suite free of charge to support her project which they seemed to know all about. They were friends of Kaz too. They hosted an international environmental website in the hotel's office and offered gracious hospitality to activist visitors from around the world.

Mick was beginning to see that Anna was part of a network of people, many of them in their early thirties, who were working on environmental projects as financial experts, legislative lobbyists, scientists, attorneys, bloggers and artists. And right now it seemed that everyone was contributing to the turtle project in some way.

He thought about turning on the TV but instead got up and went out to the rooftop moon garden. The jungle of potted plants and flowers had been chosen for their nighttime effects, Anna had explained. Flowers with white blossoms glowed in low light or released fragrance in the evening. It did smell good here, considering it was in the middle of a city of diesel trucks and full garbage cans. Straight up in the sky he could see a few stars, but nothing like the dizzy array above Cranberry Beach. Street lights gauzed the city with a pearly glow, veiling the true nature of the night. But for a city place, this rooftop garden wasn't bad.

Easing into a tippy rope hammock strung up under a vine covered arbor, he contemplated calling an old friend he hadn't seen in ages. He couldn't quite remember the name. Did he still live in the big house up the hill from the ship canal? Did he still have a room to rent out? Life in the city would be something different and far away from Cranberry Beach. But how would he pay rent? And just how much would that cost, and where would he get the money? What kind of a job would he qualify for at his age and with his limited experience? It seemed this city was meant for youngsters like Kaz, and Jeannie and Paul, movers and shakers with tech skills and advanced degrees.

Anna came into the garden talking on her phone, dropped her backpack on the floor, flopped down in a rocking chair next to the hammock and kicked off her sandals.

"Okay, I'll call you in the morning. Bye." She closed the cover on the phone and rocked quietly for a few minutes then put her feet up on a cushion. Her ankles were swollen. Before the text message from Loretta she had been tired but pleased with the day's progress.

170

But now her smile was gone and she had a faraway look and a frown that suggested she wasn't happy about what she was thinking of.

"What was so important in your email?"

She reached into her pack and pulled out a handful of papers. "It's a little disturbing." She sounded concerned in a way that indicated something bad was coming. Mick swung his legs over the edge of the hammock and sat up.

"Loretta dug up some more interesting stuff on SeaMist," she said.

"More than you showed at the meeting?"

"Yeah, though it's still a little vague at this point. She's just kind of putting two and two together. But it looks like SeaMist could have been involved in arson a few years ago."

Arson was not a word a firefighter liked to hear. "Where?"

"On the coast of Maine. A few hundred acres of timber and some vacation cabins caught fire one summer. The fire marshal thought it was intentionally set. And not only that, but it looked like the arsonist had set back-fires to spare some really picturesque forest views."

"Did they ever catch him?"

"No. There wasn't enough evidence. A professional job, according to the fire marshal."

"Who owned the land?"

"It was eleven adjacent lots, owned by different families. Most of the cabins were down by the water, backed up by a forested hill. None of the owners had anything to gain by burning down the cabins or the forest. In fact, most of the cabins weren't insured."

"What does SeaMist have to do with it?"

"Only that they came in two weeks after the fire with offers to buy up the land—for cheap. The people were still shocked and grieving and thought they would never get a better offer."

Mick was starting to get the picture. "And then SeaMist built one of their big resorts there."

"Bingo."

"They saw an opportunity and took advantage of it," Mick said.

"Or they *made* an opportunity."

"So maybe they hired an arsonist. But what does that have to do with Cranberry Beach?"

"Mick. What if SeaMist created an opportunity at Cranberry Beach?"

"What?"

"The blasting wire I found on the beach. The remote device Sean found. That could have been a detonator."

Mick tried to keep up with her tumbling logic. "You think SeaMist blasted the channel?"

"Maybe they helped the storm do it. That might be a better explanation of how it happened than just a freakish big storm."

"Uh, I don't know . . ."

"And the rescue truck. Remember the damage on the driver's door? A fan-like pattern. All those chunks of asphalt. Maybe SeaMist blew up the road right when the rescue truck was on it."

"Oh God, Anna. I don't know. If that's what happened . . ."

It seemed like a crazy idea, but on the other hand maybe there was something to it. Was that the reason for Sean's death? Had he found a detonator and taken it to the very person who had lost it? Mick felt a familiar hot stab of tears behind his eyes.

"I'm sorry," she said.

He got up and looked over the parapet at an endless procession of cars cruising for parking spots and laughing young people crowding into bars. Sean would never be one of them. Regret twisted a sob out of his throat. He fought it back, grasping for something else to talk about.

Looking up at the sky he said, "No aurora tonight—or could we even see it from here if there was one?"

Anna put her papers back in her pack and zipped it. "No—I don't think it would be visible here with all the lights."

"I liked what you said, about the tree of life."

She smiled and nodded.

"But it doesn't really help—like religion maybe would—with knowing where Sean is . . . I just can't get a handle on it."

"Some things are just too big."

172

"Yeah." He sat in a chair next to her.

"So—when you were showing me the tree of life last night and saying all the names—I was wondering. Aren't you supposed to be a scientist? I mean—you seemed more like an artist or poet or something."

Or some kind of Druid priestess, which seemed scary and weird but good in a strange way.

She laughed. "You caught me in an inspired moment. But really, it's all about love. Scientists can get bogged down with the idea that they have to be objective and distant, that they have to keep emotions and beauty out of their studies. But they love their subjects of research just as much as poets love their words and artists love their colors."

And parents love their children, Mick thought.

"That's what keeps us going when our funding flatlines or when papers get rejected. And when someone, or a team of people, makes a big discovery that advances our understanding of the world, then you know that extraordinary love went into it. Love beyond reason."

Undone again by grief, Mick went to bed and dreamed of Sean when he was a toddler, sun shining on his curly dark hair, digging with his little shovel in the sand.

13

When they arrived back at Cranberry Beach, Mick dropped Anna off at the library and parked the truck in his usual spot behind the Mercantile. The Sheriff's car sat out front. Grayson was inside, jawboning with Mick's neighbors, Ed and Rose Tilson. A twinge of shame made Mick duck his head. They all had heard his confession two nights ago.

"Hey, Mick." Ed broke off in the middle of what sounded like a long story to greet Mick with a hug. "Where'd you go? We wanted to congratulate you the other night. Took balls to say all that. You're a good guy."

Rose beamed and hugged him too. "We're not selling to SeaMist either," she said. "Who the hell wants a damned golf course in this beautiful place?"

Forgetting to finish his story, Ed picked up his bag of groceries and followed Rose out the door, waving and smiling.

Bev shuffled around the counter to hug him. "Where ya been? You didn't even leave a note."

"Oh, sorry. I just . . . had to get away for a bit. I'll be back to work tomorrow if that's okay."

"However much time you need. You just take it. No problem. But I do want you back. I need you around here, you know." She patted his arm. "We all need you."

He hugged her again and turned to the Sheriff.

"How's the investigation going?"

Grayson needed a reminder.

"Sean's murder."

"Oh. Yeah. Come on outside. We'll sit a bit."

They sat on the weathered wooden bench at the far end of the porch.

"Good news is, toxicology's back. No drugs in his system."

Though he had felt certain this would be the case, relief washed over Mick.

"The bad news is, we've got no leads. The truck was wiped clean of fingerprints which is a little strange for meth heads. They don't tend to be very detail-oriented. But that's still the direction we're looking in. Drug deal gone bad. Happens all the time."

"But he was killed somewhere else and his body was dumped at that meth lab," Mick said. "Couldn't that be a cover-up of some sort?"

"These drug lab shitheads are always screwing each other over. Market competition you know. Maybe somebody's trying to take over the local operation or something. Maybe Sean was involved in the business end of it. Could have been doing that and not using the stuff."

Mick's blood pressure ramped up, making the notch in his ear sting.

"Why just assume he was involved in drugs? Can't a person pay his debt to society and turn his life around? You saw him—he was a hard worker and a good kid."

"Mick—I don't want to have to say anything harsh about Sean. And I'd be the first to say how personable he was. And I agree he was a hard worker. But that felony drug conviction puts him in a certain category right away. And when we don't have any other plausible avenues to explore, well, we've got to go with the obvious one."

"What about the remote control device? Did you talk to Boris?"

"We talked to him. He hadn't seen Sean. Didn't know anything about any remote control device."

"Did you find it in the glove compartment of Sean's truck? That's where Stew said he saw it last."

"Nope. There wasn't anything like that in the truck."

175

"Well, there you go." Mick spread his hands, offering the self-evident. "Somebody took it—the murderer."

"Mick, calm down. There's absolutely no connection between some broken bit of beach junk and your son's death."

"What if it was a detonator?"

"A detonator? Of what?"

"Dynamite. Explosives. Plastique—I don't know what kind. But what if someone used explosives to help the sea open that channel?" He thrust his arm in the direction of the island. "And what if Sean found out about it?"

Grayson stood up, shaking his head.

"You're in outer space, buddy. There's nothing to suggest that happened. We don't have the resources in the department to follow up on that kind of wild—and may I say half-assed—suggestion, and there is no reason to even consider it." He patted Mick's shoulder. "You've lost a lot in the last few weeks. I don't blame you for grasping at straws. Somebody did kill Sean and we're looking for him. We're trying to find that crazy-assed meth cooker. I know, Meredith said they didn't know Sean. But you can't trust a meth-head to tell the truth."

He stepped off the porch and headed for his car, but turned with something else to say. "By the way, that thing you said at the meeting. Commendable. People admire you for coming clean that way. Weird time to do it, but I've seen grief make people do some strange things." He shook his head regretfully. "But not selling to SeaMist—and pulling everyone else out of it too. How the hell is this community going to survive?"

The sheriff frowned as he watched Anna walk across the street toward them, her white hair blowing in the ocean wind.

"Oh, and as for the damned Endangered Species Act," the sheriff said as he eased himself into the car, "That is one too many fucking things for my budget to absorb. The feds can police their own damned, shitty, fucking laws. I have enough homicide and drug selling and people beating up on each other to keep me and everybody in my department busy for a long, long time. The least of my problems is some little baby turtles."

176

* * *

The white midday light glanced off the choppy water as Mick rowed Anna's boat across the channel to the island. Benny stood in the bow with the breeze ruffling his ears and Anna was on the phone again.

"Guess what," she said as she closed the cover and put the phone in her backpack.

"What?"

"Tom Shepard is coming. Right now."

"That's good I guess. Did he just leave Seattle?"

"He didn't say."

"There probably won't be much daylight by the time he gets here. Why didn't he just wait until tomorrow?"

"He said he wants to look at the nest, preserve evidence, take pictures before anything gets disturbed. He said it had taken him some time to arrange transportation. So maybe he's flying."

Mick rowed, getting nowhere in his thinking about Sean's murder. What Grayson had said was frustrating. But it was true, there was no real evidence that the channel had been blasted. And there was nothing that clearly showed SeaMist would employ criminal means in their business activities. But the blackmail — was SeaMist behind that? Or just Oakley? He hadn't told the sheriff about it because Oakley and Grayson were friends. But what kind of connection did they have? Maybe they were just political friends, maybe fishing buddies . . .

A sharp noise split the air at the same time a spout of water leaped up about twenty feet to the right of the boat.

"What was that?" Anna shaded her eyes to look toward the disturbance.

There was another simultaneous fountain and cracking noise, this time closer to the boat. Mick stopped rowing and turned around to look behind him toward the island. Someone was shooting at them.

A third shot landed five feet from the bow, spraying water over Benny who ducked under Mick's seat. And a fourth went through the boat, punching a hole in the side, below the waterline, just missing Anna.

"Get down," he shouted as he dove to pull Anna down and shield her with his body. No more shots came. He peered over the gunwale, trying to see who was shooting at them. No one was visible on the beach. But Oakley's Boston Whaler was there, tied to a driftwood stump.

"Message received," Mick said. "I'll bet that's Boris somewhere up in the driftwood telling us to go away." He wondered if Oakley was there too.

Benny hopped back into the bow, sniffing toward the island and growling. Anna picked herself up from the flooding bottom of the boat. "Where's your bailing can?"

She bailed as Mick retrieved the oars and reversed their direction. The bullet hole squirted like a hose. Water sloshed eight inches deep in the bottom of the boat and increased an inch every minute. They might sink before they got back to the Cranberry Beach side if they didn't find something to plug it.

"Hey, don't you have potatoes in your grocery bag?" Mick asked.

"Yeah. Give me your knife. And keep rowing."

She whittled a potato to an appropriate size and shape and jammed it in the hole then bailed furiously.

Wind off the ocean and the channel's current pushed them toward the bay. The weight from the water they had taken on made the boat hard to maneuver. Mick struggled to keep it on course for the beach.

When Anna had gotten about half the water bailed, she sat back for a minute, breathing hard.

"The plug's holding," she said. "Let's let the current take us into the bay. We can go around and land on the other side of the island."

"Too dangerous. He'll see us."

"Well, take *me* over. You don't have to go. Just drop me off. That sonofabitch is probably digging up turtle nests. I may not be able to stop him but I can damned well be a witness."

"There's no place to land a boat over there. It's all mudflats."

She pulled her backpack on over her shoulders. "I'll go through the mud, damn it."

Benny, not heavy enough to sink in the sticky mud, trotted around them as Anna and Mick plowed through the knee-deep, black, reeking stuff. As soon as she hit the firm beach, Anna took off running through the brush, her legs crusted to the knees with thick black mud socks. She ran across the remnant of asphalt county road and dove into the brush on the other side. Benny followed silently. Mick tried to keep up, thinking she should use better surveillance, or at least look around before dashing into the open. But she was on a mission and seemed to know exactly where she was going.

She was right. Boris had found another nest near the one they had discovered two nights ago. Oakley wasn't with him. They crouched behind a pile of driftwood logs and watched him dig up the nest with a shovel.

Anna gave a hand signal and a terse, whispered command to Benny. "Stay." He sat down, ears up, watching Boris.

She unzipped a pocket of her backpack without a sound and took out her camera. They were close enough to Boris that Mick could see the sweat on the man's neck. And he could see a rifle with a scope leaning against a log.

After making a few adjustments to the tiny buttons and knobs on the camera, Anna started taking pictures. But from this viewpoint the nest wasn't clearly visible. She motioned her intent to move closer, threading through the driftwood. Mick shook his head. Just seeing Boris do this was enough, they didn't need more pictures. They could testify in court as to what they saw. But Anna was determined to thoroughly nail him.

She repeated the hand signal to Benny to stay where he was. Camera in hand, she dropped to her hands and knees. Crawling soundlessly behind a driftwood log, she positioned herself close enough to photograph the eggs as Boris scooped them into a black plastic garbage bag. Mick followed her, his heart pounding.

She motioned urgently that he should move closer. When he got to her vantage point he could see Boris lifting the shovel and repeatedly smacking it down on the sand. Some of the eggs had hatched. The tiny turtles would have clambered out of the nest and made their trek to the sea that night. But Boris was smashing them, pounding their twitching bodies to pulpy stillness.

Anna's phone announced an incoming call. Mick held his breath. Set on vibrate in her shorts pocket, it growled in the sand under her hip. Boris didn't seem to hear it over his shovel work. She silenced it, took it out, checked the display panel and showed it to Mick. The call had been from Shepard.

She switched the camera to telephoto and took some close-ups. Boris's face was masked by sunglasses and hat but she got the tattoos on his arms for positive identification. She also got pictures of the squashed babies as he shoveled them into the bag.

They backed up to a better hiding place as Boris tied a knot in the bag. He slung the strap of the rifle over his shoulder and moved away down the beach carrying the shovel and bag.

Anna and Mick changed position, keeping hidden in the driftwood, to watch Boris as he walked toward the Boston Whaler.

When he was out of hearing Anna flipped open her phone and called Shepard back.

"He's almost here," she said to Mick. "Listen. He's in a chopper."

The air pulsed with the low frequency throb of a helicopter rotor about five miles out, the sound even now recognizable as Coast Guard search and rescue.

Boris heard it too, turning to scan the sky. He tossed the bag, shovel and rifle into the boat then hurried to untie the painter.

Anna talked with Shepard, telling him what Boris had done and about the evidence he had in the boat. And that he was armed.

Tree tops bent in the rotor wash as the chopper came in low and deafening. Anna shouted into the phone.

"He can't hear me," she shouted to Mick. "He's picking up the rotor noise through my phone now."

The chopper made a pass over the channel beach and circled north.

"I don't think they see us," Anna yelled, still crouching behind the driftwood, waving her arms at the helicopter. "Or him." She thrust her arm toward Boris.

Boris, glancing several times at the chopper, pushed the boat off into the channel and started the engine.

Anna shouted into the phone a description of the boat and its direction as Boris headed into the channel toward the open sea.

The chopper appeared over the tree tops again. Boris cut his engine, grabbed the black plastic garbage bag and tossed it over the side into the channel.

Anna jumped up and ran for the open beach, waving at the chopper and pointing to Boris.

"No Anna!" She was in range of the rifle. Boris raised it to his shoulder, eye to the telescopic sight. Benny passed Mick in a white blur as they both ran toward Anna. A shot thudded into the sand in front of her. A half-second later another slammed into her body, spraying blood. She spun from the impact and crumpled. Mick heard a yelp and saw Benny fall at Anna's side. A pool of red stained his white fur and spread on the sand under him.

Mick thought he would be next.

But Boris swung the rifle up and took a shot at the chopper. He put the rifle down and slammed full power to the engine, rearing the bow up. The boat plowed through the water for a few seconds until momentum lifted the boat to plane a few inches off the surface. Then it picked up speed and was gone.

The chopper didn't follow. It turned to set down on flat ground a few hundred feet away.

Tearing his T-shirt off, Mick fell to his knees beside Anna. She was conscious but there was a lot of blood gushing out in pulses. The bullet had cut a hole through her tank top and bra strap, severing an artery in her left shoulder. He folded the T-shirt into a thick pad and pressed it onto the wound, applying pressure with the heel of his hand. Blood immediately soaked through it, spattering the sand with red dots.

"What about Benny? You've got to look after him," Anna insisted. "I'm okay. I can hold that." She reached toward her shoulder with her right hand.

Mick restrained her. "It's going to take more pressure than you can do by yourself. I'm going to have to hold it for a few more minutes. At least until Shepard gets here."

"But Benny—is he okay?" She turned her head to try to see him.

It didn't look good for the dog. He was a small animal and a very big bullet had gone through his midsection.

"Anna, he's badly injured. But he's still breathing—a little."

Blood soaked through the T-shirt and oozed between Mick's fingers. But the flow had slowed down a bit.

Tom Shepard and a coastguardsman arrived, breathing hard, after scrambling over the driftwood with a rescue basket and EMT kit. Shepard opened the kit and tore the paper off a thick stack of big gauze pads. Mick released pressure on his improvised bandage and pulled it away from the wound. Bright red blood rushed out, soaking the new pads immediately when he pressed them into place. Mick applied pressure on the stack of gauze pads as Shepard rolled a bandage tightly over it, wrapping it several times over Anna's chest, passing it around her back and both her shoulders to hold it in place during transport. The coastguardsman, a paramedic, started a saline IV.

"We're in contact with the county hospital and they're standing by," the coastguardsman said over the noise of his squawking radio. "ETA is approximately four minutes."

"Get a vet there too," Anna said. Her speech was woozy from shock and loss of blood.

The coastguardsman glanced at the lifeless-looking dog, exchanged a doubtful look with Shepard, but picked up his radio and passed on the request.

"They're on it," he said to Anna after a few seconds.

She was starting to shiver, a sign of advancing shock. They would have to transport her fast.

"Get Benny," she demanded as they lifted her into the rescue basket. Her face was pale and beaded with sweat.

Mick picked up Benny's slack body and placed it next to Anna. She cradled him with her good arm. Mick covered them both with a blanket and as Anna began a whispered prayer for Benny, they carried the basket to the helicopter.

*   *   *

In less than fifteen minutes after being shot, Anna was in a treatment bay of the emergency room surrounded by technicians cutting off her clothes, attaching monitoring gear and all talking at once. Cheryl Hopkins, in her green medical scrubs, tenderly supported Benny as she and Mick transferred him to his own gurney. She listened as she pressed a stethoscope to the dog's chest.

Anna raised her head to see him. "How is he?" Her voice trembled.

"I can hear a faint heartbeat," Cheryl said. "The vet will be here in five minutes. You concentrate on yourself now."

Cheryl put an oxygen mask over Benny's nose. His fur was soggy with blood.

Someone working on Anna growled at Mick to get out of the way. He knew he should leave the room but he couldn't.

"Mick," Anna said. "Go find Boris."

"Not until I know you're okay."

A doctor gave orders to get her into an operating room.

"I'm going to be okay. But Boris. If you go after him now he won't be able to finish what he was doing."

Tom Shepard asked Mick for help locating the evidence Boris had jettisoned in the channel, saying the sooner they went after it the better. He called the local state Fish and Wildlife officer, Pat Hughes, who picked them up in the hospital parking lot and drove them to the marina at Spencer's Landing. As they climbed into the game warden's boat and snapped on orange life jackets, Shepard explained it was standard operating procedure for National Marine Fisheries law enforcement agents to appropriate transportation from other government agencies. He had called for a Coast Guard cutter to intercept Boris but one hadn't been close enough to catch him.

"You take the Endangered Species Act pretty seriously," Mick shouted over the roar of the boat as Hughes took them at full speed across the bay to the channel.

Shepard nodded. "The sheriff's department is looking for our suspect too, on the shooting," Shepard shouted back. "I don't think he's going to get far." He frowned. "But usually our suspects don't shoot. Why would this guy take the chance of being charged with attempted murder on top of the endangered species violation?"

"He probably has more to hide than just killing turtles."

When they approached the area where Boris tossed the bag, Hughes slowed the boat. Shepard and Mick leaned over the gunwales searching the water as Hughes cruised in circles. Low tide made it easy to see the bottom.

"Hey, what's that big yellow thing?" Shepard asked.

Mick saw the huge metal treads. "That's Boris's bulldozer."

They circled around it. A corner of the bag Boris had tossed overboard was caught on the blade, preventing the current from carrying it out to sea.

Hughes throttled the engine down to keep the boat in position over the bulldozer as Mick leaned over the side with the gaff. It only took two tries to snag the black bag and lift it to the surface. Shepard secured it in the fish landing net and hauled it onboard.

"Is this what you saw him toss in the water?" Shepard asked.

"Yeah."

He untied the knot and grimaced when he looked inside.

"Okay. This is it. We'll go for search warrants for his boat and residence first thing in the morning."

"He'll get rid of everything before that."

"Get rid of what?"

184

14

Mick didn't need a search warrant to make what he could say was a social visit to Oakley's place—and Boris's apartment in Oakley's garage. Though any neighbor who saw him would have thought it strange that he parked his truck on a side road and came in the back way, thrashing through the scrub pine forest behind the garage.

He crouched under the brush for a minute to think about what he was doing. What Boris had done to Anna and Benny was clearly a cold-blooded attempt to buy himself some time. Now Mick was convinced that Boris had something seriously criminal to conceal, something way more serious than an endangered species violation. And murder was a likely reason for a man to run from law enforcement officers. Any skepticism Mick had felt before about Anna's theory was now replaced with a gut-level certainty that Boris had killed Sean to prevent exposure of his other criminal activities, which could have included blowing up the road during the storm. That would add 23 more murders to his list of criminal acts. Two of those were Don Tenney and Jimmy Whittaker, firefighters killed in the line of duty.

So Boris would be wanting to get out of the country in a hurry. Mick wondered whether he had been paid to carry out these criminal acts and whether it was also his job, before he left, to clean up any evidence that might implicate SeaMist.

If Anna and Loretta were right about SeaMist creating an opportunity here at Cranberry Beach, there would be plenty of evidence to destroy before the federal investigation got near it. And Shepard had assured him his inquiry into Boris's violation of the

Endangered Species Act would extend as far as necessary into SeaMist's corporate activities. If SeaMist had directed Boris to dig up the turtle nests, the corporation would be subject to criminal indictments and some very big fines. Whatever other wrongdoing was uncovered in the investigation would be prosecuted by other governmental agencies. And a host of conservation organizations would be more than willing to bring civil lawsuits against SeaMist. Not to mention the civil suits that could be brought by peninsula landowners and families of the flood victims.

But regardless of any contractual obligations to SeaMist, it would be in Boris's personal best interest to get rid of the evidence. The attempted murder of Anna and the endangered species violation might not be enough to get him extradited back to the U.S. from whatever foreign country he might flee to. But blowing up the road, causing the deaths of all those people and killing Sean to cover it up might.

Mick shuddered. If Boris saw him here, he wouldn't hesitate to shoot him too. But his anger over what Boris had done to Anna and Benny had overcome his instinct for self-preservation. And this could be his only chance to prove Sean's innocence. By the time the official search warrants were served Boris would be long gone and nothing would remain to tell the true story of Sean's death.

Grayson had ordered his deputies to patrol the few nearby places where Boris might beach or dock Oakley's boat. The Coast Guard was looking for it too, and also patrolling the beach with the idea that Boris had to come ashore some time and they could easily catch him then. But Mick had recently acquired a new respect for the chilling efficiency of the man he had previously seen as nothing more than a bad-tempered cartoon character. Boris Badenov would not be easy to catch and he would definitely be back here—soon.

Mick figured he had maybe an hour. Maybe five minutes. It was crazy to put himself in danger like this without any way to defend himself. As far as he could see, no deputy had yet been assigned to watch Oakley's house. And he didn't really have a plan other than to sneak in and look for something that might be evidence. Maybe he could take something away, something like a stick of

186

dynamite or maybe a broken remote control device with Russian lettering.

He imagined how Sean must have parked his truck in the driveway, curious about what must have seemed to him an exotic find. He would have approached Boris in a friendly, innocent way. Had he even known why he was murdered?

And had Oakley been there?

The thought turned his stomach.

Mick eased around the side of the big, two-story garage. He looked in a window. No cars were parked inside. None were in the driveway either.

He could see a room through a half-open door in the back of the garage. There was an easy chair and a bed. This must be Boris's apartment. Mick tried a side door which was locked. Inching around to the far side of the garage he peeked through slanting venetian blinds into a storage room stacked with wooden crates.

The sliding window to this room wasn't locked. He opened it and lifted the dusty blinds. It was dark inside except where a shaft of light brushed across some lettering on the crates. He would have to go in to really see what was there.

With his heart pounding in his throat, he boosted himself up to the window sill and scrambled over it. He dismounted clumsily, falling over crates stacked under the window. Clattering to the floor he lay still, shocked at the amount of noise he had made, expecting to see the door open and a firearm aimed at his forehead.

Nothing happened. He stood up cautiously and looked around. The crates were labeled in what looked like Cyrillic and decorated with a series of graphic symbols. He squatted to get a closer look. They seemed to be typical shipping cautions. A picture of stylized glassware and a word beneath it that must have meant *fragile*. Another indicated *this side up*. He saw the universal circle and slash symbols for no smoking and no open flame.

And a yellow triangle with diagonal black marks which took a minute to fully comprehend. It pictured a small round object in the lower left corner, broken open and ejecting chunks of high energy debris. Explosives.

187

There were about fifteen of those in the room.

A workbench against the wall was piled with rolls of wire, small electrical components, clocks, electronic devices, blasting caps and a coil of detonating cord like the piece Anna had found on the beach. Several glass jugs filled with liquids sat in padded boxes along one wall.

In a trash can beside the workbench Mick found a broken gray plastic housing with a knob in the center of it and part of an antenna sticking out the top. Cyrillic lettering labeled it and sand caked its insides. He found a paper towel and picked the device up with it, hoping to preserve fingerprints for forensic analysis. Maybe Sean's would be on it. He dropped it into what seemed a reasonably clean plastic grocery bag he also found in the trash can and put it in his back pocket.

Sliding the window shut, he slipped out of the room and crossed the garage floor.

Mick looked into the apartment. Boris clearly wasn't the domestic sort. In the kitchenette, the tiny counter and sink were piled with empty take-out boxes. The bed was unmade and a stack of porn videos occupied the easy chair. Several boxes of ammunition were stacked on the floor and a high powered rifle with a telescopic sight leaned in the corner. It looked like the one Boris had used to shoot Anna and Benny. So Boris had already been home. Maybe he was across the drive at Oakley's house, but if so where was his SUV? Mick picked up the rifle and saw *Kalashnikov* stamped on the stock. He had seen a picture of one like it in a magazine. It was a sniper's rifle, a few decades old, but still highly effective in the right hands. It was probably the weapon Boris had used to kill Sean. Mick wrapped it in a shirt, carried it out through the side door of the garage, and ran into the woods with it.

When he had gotten a safe distance into the scrub pines he stopped. A thought nagged at him. He had acquired this evidence illegally. Would it be useless in convicting Sean's killer? Maybe he shouldn't have taken it. But at least it would be available to law enforcement this way. It wouldn't be if Boris had the opportunity to dispose of it.

What else would Boris try to get rid of? The explosives. And anything else that would implicate SeaMist.

And what about Oakley's role? Mick's mission wasn't complete. At the very least he had to find out how deeply Oakley was involved.

Concealing the remote control device and gun under a pile of bracken, Mick crept back to the edge of the brush and watched Oakley's house. The driveway remained empty of cars. He could see no motion in the house.

He ran across the back yard to the back door of the house and watched the wheel on the electric meter beside the door. It barely moved which was a good sign. No one was inside doing something that required electricity like watching TV or heating something in the microwave. He listened at the door and heard nothing then tried the handle. It wasn't locked.

Mick had no idea what he was looking for. He wandered around inside Oakley's house, perplexed and jumpy. It was spacious but nearly as devoid of domesticity as Boris's apartment. He pushed open what seemed to be a bedroom door and found a small office. One window set high in the wall let in a little light. There was a typical bedroom clothes closet with folding doors. A desk held a computer and a rats nest of electronic gear and cables.

A thick pile of architectural drawings lay on a table. Mick shuffled through them. Some looked like the ones on the video SeaMist had shown at the meeting. They pictured site plans and floor plans for individual buildings or clusters of buildings. Some were site plans for the entire island. Each sheet was identified in the lower right corner with the SeaMist logo, an architect's official stamp and initials, and information about the drawing. And the date.

The drawing at the bottom of the pile was dated two years ago.

Mick thought it must have been a mistake. He pulled the sheet out and laid it on top of the pile. It was a site plan of the island but it looked different from the other site plans. The contour of the south end of the island where the channel cut through was depicted as angling more sharply to the southeast than it did in reality. And the channel was shown as half the width it really was.

He dug further in the pile of drawings and pulled out an aerial photo of the peninsula, taken before the breach. His house and pastures were clearly visible. A black line penned across the middle of the photo more or less delineated the area of the new channel. Arrows pointed out the low-lying ground of Mick's cranberry bogs on the bay side and the course of Decker Creek on the ocean side.

He picked up the drawing and compared angles with the lines drawn on the photo. What was sketched on the photo corresponded to the shape that was drawn two years ago for the south end of the new island resort.

Anger climbed up his neck and throbbed in the notch of his ear. It was clear that SeaMist had planned the resort many months ago and had breached the peninsula as part of a deliberate plan. And he was holding what in a court of law would amount to a smoking gun. If he could get it out of Oakley's house before Boris—or Oakley—got back to destroy it. It would be a job for the lawyers to battle out the legality of how it had been obtained.

He rolled the photo and the architect's drawing together and snapped a rubber band around it.

A car door slammed in the driveway.

Oakley shouted something, nearly at the front door. There wasn't time to dash through the kitchen and out the back door before Oakley saw him.

So he dove into the closet. And immediately kicked himself for not remembering whether the closet door had been open a crack or closed tightly. Shit. He decided to leave it open an inch and pressed himself into a corner clutching the rolled drawing and photo. A little light came in. Several cardboard boxes labeled with a printer's logo were stacked in the closet's other corner. It looked like copies of the SeaMist prospectus. Maybe this closet was a really dumb place to hide if they were going to destroy everything related to SeaMist. But they wouldn't need to get rid of the stuff that was already public. Maybe they would just come in and take the drawings away, and the computer. Nothing important was in the closet.

The front door banged open and Mick heard Boris shouting orders to Oakley. In English. The office door opened a second later and both men came in wrangling.

"It's all your fault you stupid bastard," Oakley raged. "We're toast and it's all because of you."

"Never mind about past," Boris growled. "Think of future. Erase everything here and start over somewhere else. Easy. Now help with this."

There was a sound of grunting exertion, then of something heavy being slid up against the closet doors, pushing them completely shut.

"Take hand truck and get the rest," Boris ordered.

"Hell no. I don't want to touch that stuff."

"Sissy boy. Afraid? Don't worry. Is stable until detonate. Then blooey." Boris laughed. "Go get it. You said we're in hurry."

Mick thought that getting into this closet was about the stupidest thing he had ever done. He would have to think of some way to get out, fast. He soundlessly patted around in the now pitch dark closet. There was no rod for hanging clothes but there was a shelf above his head supported by metal angle brackets. He got his knife out of his pocket, folded out the screwdriver and began to silently undo the screws that fastened one of the brackets.

Oakley came back and they stacked more of the explosives crates around the room.

"What the hell were you thinking?" Oakley said, breathing hard. "Why the *hell* did you shoot at those people?"

"Never mind. My business."

"No. Not just your business. You *exposed* us. Why didn't you just get rid of those damned turtle nests like Younger told you to and get out of there?"

"I think that lady saw me. Coast Guard too."

Oakley sputtered a string of curses.

"You know," he said. "You're what we call a loose cannon. Do you have that phrase in Russian?"

Boris hummed as he worked, presumably putting together the wiring that would detonate all those explosives.

"You could have talked yourself out of a lot of problems. Like Sean Mahoney. You could have made something up and he would have gone away happy and never thought about it again. But you just up and shoot him. And then I have to deal with it. And now you shoot someone else and you've blown the whole project. SeaMist could have done something about the turtle thing. Lawyers. Bribes. Whatever. But you do something that gets everybody mad and then they start sniffing around."

"Sorry. Think about future."

Oakley was on a tirade. "And about blowing up the road. Who the hell told you to do that? We were supposed to work that breach slowly, over four years. A little bit at a time, just helping along the natural erosion by moving the sand with the bulldozer. Doing a little blasting here and there. But you had to do something spectacular. A lot of people *died*."

Mick imagined Boris shrugging.

Oakley, on a roll, kept ranting. "Frankly, I don't care if you *are* a fucking explosives expert. You don't have *judgement* man. You have totally screwed us up."

"Go get more boxes."

"Shit." Oakley kicked the door for emphasis on his way out.

Mick had the bracket off now and it lay on the floor beside him. He folded the screwdriver away and opened out his biggest blade. He had kept it sharp, honing it during quiet times at the Mercantile. So when he pressed it into the gypsum wallboard in the back of the closet the knife went in easily and silently.

Oakley returned, announcing, as they stacked them, that this was all the boxes.

"Okay," Boris said. "Everything out of store room?"

"Yeah," Oakley snarled.

"Kalashnikov."

"It wasn't in your closet."

192

"Go look again. And turn off pilot lights. Then break propane valve."

"Why do that?"

"Look like accident," Boris chuckled. "Make bigger boom."

Mick used his knife to slice through the tough paper surface of the wallboard and partly through the three-quarter-inch thickness of plaster. Then he jimmied the metal bracket into the scored lines to pry a hole through to the stud space. Peeling away handfuls of the wallboard, he cleared a passage into the stud space between the closet and the adjoining master bedroom. Then he plunged his knife into the back of the wallboard that covered the other side.

Boris seemed to be busy in the living room and Mick could hear Oakley banging at the valve where the propane line came into the kitchen. Now was a good time to break through into the bedroom. He hoped nothing big was in the way.

He pushed with his shoulder at the opening he had started between the wooden studs. The wallboard gave way with a muffled thump. Chunks of it scattered on the carpeted floor. Lucky. He had missed by a few inches dead-ending into the back of an oak armoire.

Mick squeezed through into Oakley's master bedroom carrying the roll of drawings. He could hear Boris humming as he worked in the living room.

Oakley's banging was replaced by the shriek of propane escaping from the broken valve. The sulfurous vapor drifted through the kitchen and across the floor. In a few minutes the house would be full of it.

Mick's route to safety was ten steps away, through the French doors that opened from the bedroom onto the back patio.

He could hear Oakley in the living room now. "Shit, man. I don't *know* where your fucking Kalashnikov is."

Boris responded angrily in a mix of Russian and English.

"Hell, it's probably in the garage somewhere," Oakley said. "Why didn't we just haul the computer and everything over there? It would have been easier to blow up the garage to get rid of all your toys and shit."

"Royal pain in ass," Boris growled.

"It's probably in your car or something. But *you* can fucking go and get it."

"Too much gas now. Too late for firearm."

Mick thought now would be the time to run for it. A knee-deep fog of propane vapor floated through the house. But it seemed Oakley didn't get the significance of Boris's last statement.

"See?" Oakley said, exasperated. "This is a perfect example of the half-assed way you work. You don't plan ahead or think things through."

"Give me hammer."

"What hammer? Where the hell is it?"

"There, in box."

"Oh. Okay, here. But we'll find the Kalashnikov later and . . . ."

A sickening thud ended Oakley's chatter. The front door closed. Mick saw Boris through the bedroom window, running toward the garage.

He was probably taking one last look in the garage for the gun. That meant there would be a few more minutes before the explosion—or a few seconds. And there was a chance Oakley was still alive.

The thought that Oakley would be an essential witness to Sean's murder and SeaMist's other crimes never occurred to Mick as he jammed the drawings under his belt. Emergency training focused his mind on the task at hand, overriding the instinctive fear response of being in a dangerous situation. Someone else might have made the judgement that Oakley wasn't worth the risk of losing his own life. But that never entered Mick's mind either.

He took a deep breath and held it as he dove into the living room and reached into the thick propane fog for a grip on Oakley's jacket. He dragged the unconscious man into the bedroom and catching another sulfurous breath, he heaved Oakley up onto his shoulders in a fireman carry and burst out the French doors.

He caught a glimpse of Boris running for his SUV. Lunging across the back yard and into the pines, Mick heard the car's wheels skid in the gravel as Boris gunned it out of the driveway.

Oakley was a dead weight but Mick staggered on, carrying him into the woods as far as he could before the explosion sprawled him face down in the pine needles and moss.

15

Two weeks after Boris shot her, Mick was answering Anna's questions as he rowed her and Benny across the channel.

"Tom Shepard was aboard a Coast Guard cutter that caught up with Boris about twenty miles out. That was an hour after he blew up Oakley's house. They think he was heading for a Russian fishing boat."

The day Anna had been discharged from the hospital she had gone to Newport to verify several turtle nests discovered on the beaches there. Now, with her arm in a sling buckled to her midriff, she had returned to Cranberry Beach for physical therapy on her shoulder to restore her range of motion.

"Did he put up a fight?"

"Yeah. But the cutter had more firepower than he did. They shot a big hole in Oakley's boat."

Anna laughed. "Did it sink?"

"Enough to make him give up. He's in federal detention now. Your photos were enough to convince the magistrate to hold him on the endangered species violations. They're working on more charges too. Immigration as well as murder, attempted murder and resisting arrest. And blowing up the road. I heard SeaMist would have paid just about anything to get him out of jail. And out of the country. But the feds consider him a flight risk. So no bail."

Anna ruffled Benny's ears and kissed the top of his head. "Good," she said to the dog. "Boris needs to be locked up. Doesn't he?"

Benny gave her face a lick then resumed his posture of alert attention as he gazed toward the island. He sat in Anna's lap, still bandaged around his middle. Boris's bullet had missed all major organs and big blood vessels and Benny had received excellent veterinary care.

"What about Oakley?" Anna asked.

"Recovering. And talking."

"That must be helpful for Shepard's investigation."

"You bet it is," Mick said, "Tom thinks he has a good case against SeaMist of blatant, deliberate violation of endangered species laws. He tells me a few of these kinds of cases against corporations have recently pulled down huge fines. And the interesting part is that in the past the fines went into the federal treasury where they could be used anywhere in the general budget. But now corporations are being sentenced to pay their fines directly to mitigation banks — like ours."

"Hah." Anna grinned. "How perfectly appropriate. They'll end up paying big bucks for the land they were trying to steal. And that's only the beginning of their troubles."

Mick rowed, enjoying the warm breeze. November on the peninsula in past years had always been wet, cold and miserable. This year it felt more like the sunny, dry climate of California. A few scientists were now saying this could be how global warming was going to manifest itself in the Pacific Northwest. And they were backing off what a few months ago had been the generally accepted scientific view that climate change was a gradual process. It was coming on abruptly and in some places catastrophically. Glacier melt had surged all over the world, sending huge amounts of fresh water into the oceans, seriously changing salinity and interrupting currents. Whole south Pacific islands were now being inundated as rapid warming made sea levels rise.

In the past, geologists had assured the peninsula community that any rise in sea level along the Pacific Northwest coast would be offset by the ongoing lifting of tectonic plates. But they were backing off that too. In only one year the average high tide mark had advanced inland on the peninsula by ten feet.

And now another storm was headed for the coast. The weather service, blindsided last summer by a kind of storm not described in the textbooks, wasn't going to take any chances this time. They had recommended evacuation of low-lying coastal areas early enough to avoid another disaster.

The only hint Mick could see of what was coming in the next twenty-four hours was a high, thin cloud that veiled the sun with rainbow spots, what Anna called sun dogs. And an ocean swell that rolled through the channel, lifting the boat as he rowed. It recalled the queasy sensation of floating on the storm surge in the Suburban. But this time he would be able help Anna gather her things from her campsite in the driftwood and get her to safety off the peninsula well before the storm.

At the campsite they made a pile of things to take back to Cranberry Beach. Her sleeping bag and tent. The half bottle of Jack Daniel's. A few cans of food, her collapsible water container, camp stove and cooking pots.

The boat and camping gear would probably be safe at the Mercantile during the storm, but Anna and Benny planned to evacuate with Bev to a relative's house in Astoria for the night. Mick would stay in Cranberry Beach with other emergency personnel to protect property and the lives of those who refused to go.

The emergency band radio on his hip squawked. He thumbed up the volume to listen to the call. A car wreck on the other side of the bay, out of the Cranberry Beach fire district.

"Hey," Anna said. "I hear you made chief. Congratulations."

"Nothing much different from what I was doing before. But now I get $420 a month from the county."

Actually, it meant more to him than he could say. Wally and Irmalene had organized an avalanche of letters and phone calls recommending Mick for the position opened up by Oakley's arrest. The county emergency services director had waived—or ignored—the usual human resources hiring procedures, bypassed the interim stage and appointed him permanent chief.

"I prefer to leave my campsite the way I found it," Anna said. "But we can't carry all of these dishes and cushions in the boat."

Mick laughed. "Maybe you should walk down the beach, throwing it all back where you found it. But then I'd have to pick it up later with the rest of the storm junk. It's just as well left here."

"You're going to clean up the beach?"

"Yeah. Part of making the island a wildlife sanctuary. We're going to clear out as much of the storm debris as we can without disturbing habitat. At least on the beach. And we're looking at what to do with the houses. But that's a long-range project."

"Sounds like a lot of work."

"Maybe not as much as SeaMist promised to Cranberry Beach. But it'll be a nice year or so of income for several people around here."

"And for you?"

"It's a permanent job. Kaz hired me to look after the daily operations out here. There'll be lots to do. So far they've found five other endangered species on the island including two kinds of mud critters on the bay side. So that expands the scope of the conservation bank beyond just sea turtles. And the whole north point is going to be restored to wetland for migratory birds."

"Let's walk a bit before we go," Anna suggested after they had loaded everything into the boat.

Benny waddled along beside them, his usual jaunty gait hindered by his bandages. He angled off to the upper beach, sniffing vigorously around in the sand.

Anna shaded her eyes to watch him. "I think he might be able to smell turtle nests."

Benny whined and pawed at the sand until Anna and Mick got there.

"Look," Anna said. "These parallel marks in the sand look like turtle tracks."

"Are you doing to dig and see if it's a nest?"

"No. I don't want to harm it."

Mick looked at the sky. A thick, curdled-looking cloud was bearing down from the southwest. "If this storm is anything like the last one, this nest isn't going to survive."

"We can't protect them from storms. It's part of the covenant all living beings have with the earth. That there will be violence and death. But it's balanced out by abundant life."

"How's that?"

She gestured to the nest. "A sea turtle lays a hundred eggs. Fifty of them might hatch. Perhaps twenty die before they reach the sea. Maybe twenty-nine more become food for something else before they can grow up. But there's one more turtle to crawl up on the land and dig a nest. Somewhere deep in the molecules of its DNA, every living thing understands that's how it works. So that's why it's such a crime when humans destroy whole species of living beings. It's a crime against the covenant we're all bound by. Humans have gotten the idea that we stand outside of that covenant. But it's not so and we're going to be reminded of that."

Mick thought of Boris crushing the baby turtles. It had been deliberate and premeditated murder, as it had been when he killed Sean. But the news Mick had heard from Sandy yesterday and hadn't yet absorbed—was that the balance Anna was talking about?

She continued speaking passionately as if it were no longer Mick she was addressing but a congregation of thousands.

"We humans can barely grasp the complexity of life. Like how these turtles came to nest on this beach. Scientists like to say that the mechanisms have yet to be discovered. They know sea turtles navigate using parts of their brains attuned to small variations in the earth's magnetic field. Maybe they'll discover that the magnetic field shifted a little this summer. But they'll never really understand *why* that happened."

She gazed at the ocean for a few minutes.

"Unless that covenant involves more than we think it does. What if what we call nature is more than a hugely complex but ultimately mechanistic set of causes and effects? What if there's an intelligence, a *presence*? What if some*one* moved the turtles?"

She stopped and regarded Mick as if expecting some kind of answer.

"Sounds like religion I guess."

200

"More like myth, the foundation of religion. The old myth of the patriarchal gods says the advancement of knowledge is power, a continuation of the naming of creatures that Adam began in Eden. Name it, know it and have power over it. Now, through knowledge, humans have the power to erase species, to change the climate, to destroy habitats. So if those are crimes against the covenant of living on the earth, I wonder if humans are going to be prosecuted. And whether that some*one* believes in capital punishment."

A dismal, defeating thought. "Maybe that someone believes in mercy."

Anna smiled. "We can only hope."

She found a stick and pushed it into the sand near the turtle nest saying maybe the sea wouldn't take it in the storm and this marker would help them find it later.

Anna took off her sandals. Walking barefoot in the warm sand she said, "I'm so glad to be alive."

The bullet had hit a major artery. She could have died on the beach if the helicopter transport hadn't been right there.

"And Benny's alive too." She stopped and stretched out her hands, palms up and eyes closed in a gesture of prayer. "Thank you," she murmured.

Sean was not alive. No mercy there.

"I don't get religion," he said.

"I don't either. All I can do is be grateful for life. And see myself in the context of something bigger. One tiny — and beloved — creature in the whole incredible, mysterious web of existence."

Mick's skepticism of Anna's offbeat spirituality had long ago burned away. Now he wanted to believe as she did. But he still groped in the dark, stumbling over fragments of religious dogma he had unconsciously absorbed even as he rejected them over the years.

"What does it mean," he asked, "that my son died . . ." grief caught at his throat, "and yesterday Sandy told me she's pregnant with his child?"

Anna smiled and her blue eyes welled up with tears. "I don't know what it means. But it's good."

"Sandy's parents are going to use the money they get from the conservation bank to build a new marina at Cranberry Beach," Mick said. "They're planning to build a nice big apartment there too. Sandy and the baby will live with them."

"Where are you going to live?" Anna asked.

"I'm fine at the Mercantile. It's all I need. All I want."

"I need to find a short term rental while I do the physical therapy for my shoulder," Anna said. "Or I could go back to Newport and get PT there. But I do love it here."

"Bev has a guest room at the Mercantile. She would probably rent it to you for a little while."

"I'm thinking long term too, quitting my job at the National Marine Fisheries. I'm going to be consulting on sea turtle habitat for companies doing environmental impact studies. A couple of calls have come in already."

"Do you want to call Cranberry Beach home?"

She smiled and nodded. "Yes, I'd like to live here."

The conservation bank had paid Mick a fair price for his land, including what was now under water. He had more money than he ever hoped for. And he had more jobs than he had ever imagined. He was investing some of his money and a lot of time helping a young family start up a small business. Ecotourism. A concept Cranberry Beach would have scoffed at before. But people were coming from all over, asking to see the turtles.

And he had another idea too.

"Anna, I'd like to build you a house."

She didn't answer right away.

"I have enough money to invest in building a rental and I can't think of anyone I'd like better to rent it to."

She raised a questioning eyebrow and started to shake her head. Disappointment surprised him. He enjoyed her company more than he could admit.

"Mick, I'm going to be traveling a lot, especially in the next few years. I don't need a whole house."

"Well, wait. This is my idea. I want to build something for the tourists who come to see the turtles. The ecotourists. For their

202

vacations. I was thinking it could be a houseboat moored at the new marina. And there would be rooms just for you and rooms for vacationers. And a place for their kayaks on the deck."

"Hmmm. And a place for my kayak?"

"Yeah."

"That might work."

"And if the bay floods again the houseboat will float," Mick said, smiling like the sun coming out.

Anna grinned. "And if it gets tossed onto the land in a big storm, we can just push it back into the bay."

"We could paint it blue. A blue houseboat. Like your dream."

Mick rowed them back to Cranberry Beach through channel water now choppy with the rising wind. A quarter mile away in the ocean surf, currents and wave action scooped up sand and churned it into suspension. The turbid water flowed toward the bay on the high tide. One by one, sand particles sifted down over the channel bottom, burying the yellow bulldozer, and in their own slow geological time mending the breach.

Many thanks to agents of the NOAA Office for Law Enforcement for information on procedures for investigating endangered species crimes, to Angela Smith and Catherine Minnig of the Seattle Aquarium Sea Turtle Rehabilitation Facility, and to fisheries biologist, Craig Rose. Thanks also to Amy Rader Eames and Sue Baldwin for their excellent copy editing and to Chris Peterson for reading and encouragement. I'm grateful to my mom, Shirley Root, EMT (Retired), North Olympia Volunteer Fire Department for details about emergency medical treatment. And to Jim Clark, Chuck Fowler and Randy Morris of the Thomas Berry Study Group for their contributions to the ecophilosophical aspects of this book. But most of all I'm grateful for my family, for their love and unconditional support of my creative endeavors, especially my dad, Eddie Root, who generously and wholeheartedly served his community as Assistant Fire Chief of the North Olympia Volunteer Fire Department.

32526768R00117

Made in the USA
San Bernardino, CA
08 April 2016